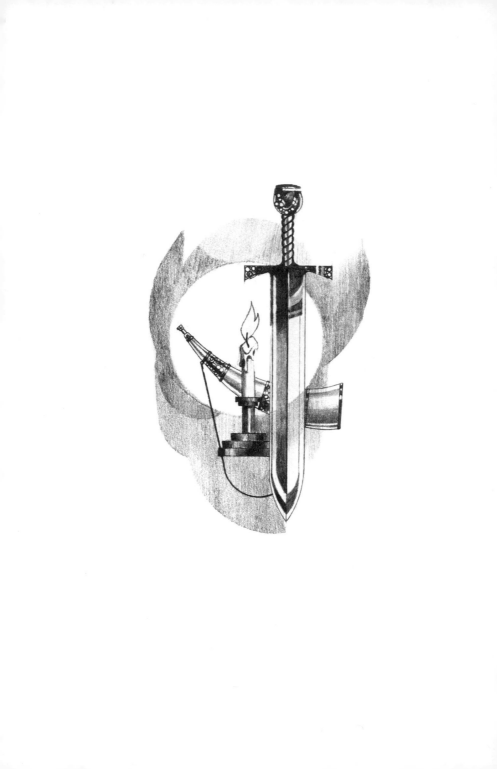

Magician's Bane

Book One of The Legends of Eorthe

By

Charles Beamer

THOMAS NELSON PUBLISHERS
Nashville

Magician's Bane

Cover and text illustrations are by Don Pallarito

Library of Congress Cataloging in Publication Data

Beamer, Charles.
  Magician's bane.

  (His Legends of Eorthe; book 1)
  SUMMARY: Waymond the magician takes 13-year-old Jodi and her 9-year-old brother Martin to the Land of the King where their help is needed in the struggle of goodness against evil.
  [1. Fantasy] I. Title. II. Series.
PZ7.B365Le   1980,   bk.1   [Fic]   79-28151
ISBN 0-8407-5193-1

To:
Alice
Jodi
Shannon
George
Mary
Joe
Chris

Contents

Open a window,
Open a door;
Let hope spring free,
Then run for more.
CB

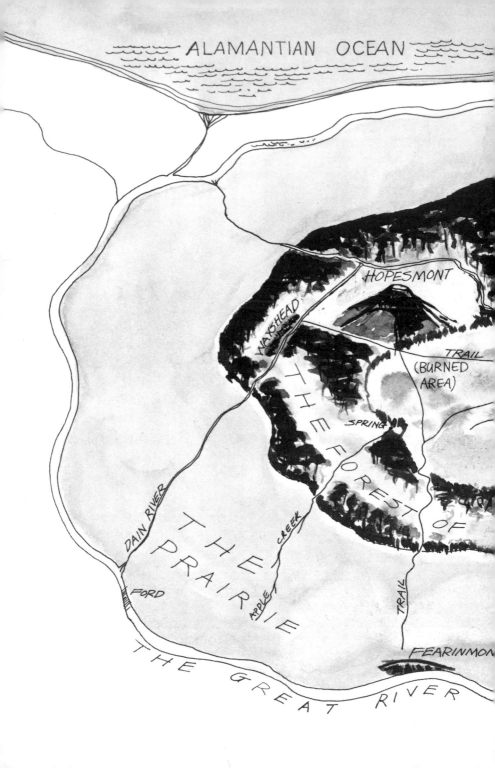

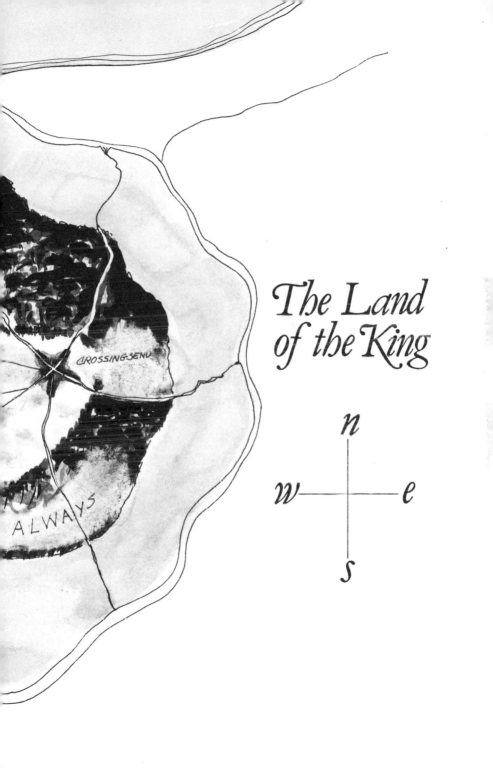

Chapter 1

A Knock on the Door

"*L*et's do something!" Martin Westphall pleaded. He leaned on his sister's bed and turned his soulful blue eyes upon her.

She laid aside the book she was reading and reached over to turn down the volume of her record player. "I don't want to," she said icily. She pushed her light brown hair away from her eyes and looked at the posters on the walls of her room.

Martin squirmed. "Oh, you never want to do anything. Come on, Jodi, let's go work on the clubhouse or play pirates or army or *something!*"

Jodi, a dignified thirteen-year-old, practically sneered at her nine-year-old brother. "That's baby stuff. If we do anything, let's play hospital." She sat up with unusual eagerness, and her eyes got a dreamy look. "We could pretend that an epidemic was ravishing the world—some strange disease. I could be the doctor who finds a cure, and you could be the nurse who gives all the children shots and saves their lives."

"Why can't I be the doctor?" Martin pouted, lying across her bed. "You're the one who wants to be a nurse, so let me be the doctor!"

Jodi picked up her book with a bored look. "If

you're going to argue with me, I don't want to play. Besides, I'd rather read."

"Oh, all you ever do is lie in here and read. Just 'cause you're scared to go outside . . ."

"I am not!" Jodi cried, insulted.

"You are! Martin argued. "You almost never go out—and Mom and Dad . . ."

"Mom and *Richard*," Jodi corrected, unwilling to call her stepfather by anything but his first name.

"Mom and *Dad* told us we could do anything we wanted to or go anywhere we wanted to as long as nobody got hurt, and as long as we let them know where we are and about when we'll be back. So come on, let's . . ."

"No!" Jodi said sharply. "I'm tired of playing with you. I have to tell you *everything* to do and . . ."

"You do not," Martin pouted. He stuck out his tongue at her.

Jodi laughed at him. "Oh yeah? Well, if I watch television, so do you. And you eat only the same things I eat, and if you don't know the answer to some question, who do you ask?"

"Not always," Martin objected. His pleading look returned. "Come on, let's at least go visit somebody . . . maybe old Mrs. Harkess and that foster child she took in."

Jodi considered it, then shook her head. "No," she said thoughtfully. "I'm tired of trying to be nice to people; they're mean."

"Mrs. Harkess isn't!" Martin snapped. "Just because you let some people hurt your feelings doesn't mean . . ."

"Leave . . . me . . . alone!" Jodi said, her gray-blue eyes flashing a warning.

Martin pressed his point like a swordsman with a

villain on the run. "Just because you don't think Mom and *Dad* love you enough."

Jodi sat upright and slammed shut her book. Her teeth were clenched, and her expression was filled with anger. "See?" she demanded. "That's what I get for telling you anything! You're mean like the rest of them!"

He saw that she truly was hurt, so he quickly said, "Gee, I'm sorry, Jodi. I just wanted you to play something."

She sighed. "All right. How about a game of Monopoly?"

"Aw, I don't want to play that. You always beat me," Martin hedged.

"It's that or nothing," Jodi said definitely.

So, they got out the board and pieces and began to play. Jodi was the realtor, and Martin was the banker because he was quick with numbers. And as they played they fought, as was their habit when they were stuck at home together.

Jodi and Martin lived in a town that was neither small nor large. It was a town they thought to be quite ordinary. There was a courthouse square, a college nearby, and some small factories on the edge of town. Three highways and a railroad ran through their town and led out through surrounding farms and ranches to points unknown to the Westphall children. Beyond the ranches, before one came to other towns, was a river. Across the river was an area of wilder land that civilization had not quite conquered.

It was from that wilder land that a King's magician came that very afternoon. He came unnoticed by the ordinary townspeople and walked unheeded up the ordinary streets to the ordinary white house on the ordinary block where Jodi and Martin Westphall lived. From that point on, almost nothing was ordinary.

When the knock came on the front door of the Westphall house, Jodi had just gotten a monopoly on the yellow properties and was about to buy four houses. So, as she went to the door, she was annoyed at having to talk with a visitor. She peered out the window beside the front door to see who might be persistently knocking: "Knock-knock-knock . . . knockknockknock!"

"Who are you?" she asked through the screen over the open window.

"My name is Waymond."

Jodi pursed her lips. "That doesn't tell me much. Waymond who?"

"Jodi Kay Westphall, I am Waymond, a King's magician!"

Jodi blinked in surprise. "How did you know my name?"

"Oh, I know much more than your name."

"Such as?" Jodi asked in as cold a tone as she could muster.

"Such as the fact that, though others may not see or believe it, you are a person who would very, *very* much like to be brave."

Jodi frowned; a stranger had no right to know that. Nor did he have any right to be interrupting her afternoon of beating Martin at Monopoly, even if he did sound kind and gentle. "Come back after 5:30 when my parents are home," she said emphatically, turning away.

"No, sorry, but that won't do at all," the stranger said, bending down to peer inside. "We need your help *now*."

She ignored what he said—because people often came by asking for donations to various causes—and stared silently out at him. He appeared to be a pleasant man, neither young nor old. He had long, curly brown hair and beard, brown eyes that sparkled, and coarse, loose fitting clothing. *He certainly doesn't look like a fund raiser*, she thought. She saw that he wore boots with high tops folded down. She noticed further that he carried a carpetbag in his left hand, and that in his right hand was a tall, curiously carved staff.

"Please, we need your help," he repeated.

"No!" Jodi snapped, frightened by his persistence. She heard Martin come up behind her.

"Who is it?" Martin whispered, bending down beside Jodi to peek around her at the stranger. For some reason Martin began to smile.

"It's no one," Jodi said. To the man outside she added, "Go away or I'll call the police! They'll take away your license to ask for . . ."

"Oh, but I'm not asking you to give anything except your time and courage," the stranger smiled, straightening. "And I'm *offering* you something. You see, I also know for a fact that you wish you could be more loved. And, though you may not realize it, your brother shares that wish." He bent down and winked one sparkling brown eye at Martin.

Martin was curious, but Jodi was bothered to the point of crying. Martin, despite his interest, saw the troubled look on his sister's face and became quite angry. "You go away!" he shouted out the window. "You've upset my sister!"

"I'm sorry," Waymond said gently, "but sometimes a bit of discomfort is necessary. If I don't cause you a bit of discomfort now, you and Jodi might continue to grow up believing nobody loves you enough. You might also continue to grow up thinking that neither of you truly can be brave! So, I want you to meet a very dear friend of mine—the King. He and I have need of

17

you and Jodi, and what you'll get will be far more than what you'll be asked to give."

Before Martin could ask who the King might be, Jodi sadly said, "No one needs us. Mom and Richard do everything around here. And . . ."

"I know you don't think they need you. But they do . . . and so do I! So does the King I serve!"

"For what?" Jodi asked cautiously.

"For an adventure involving goodness against evil."

"Oh, phooey!" Jodi snapped. But her curiosity was aroused. *Did such adventures still really happen?* she wondered hopefully.

As though he had read her thoughts, Waymond stamped his staff on the porch with a *thunk!* "Come with me and you shall see."

For an instant, Jodi was tempted to say yes . . . but she stopped herself and folded her arms. "No. Go find someone else. There are plenty of other children. Besides, it's too hot to go out. We'd just get all sweaty and tired and . . . and how do we know we can trust you?"

Waymond bent down beside the window in full view. The tip of his brown beard moved up and down as he earnestly said, "It's about some of those other children—and a very special place—that I've come. I know you don't know me, but please at least consider my problem. I am a magician, a King's magician, one of very few who remain. Now, I do not make ladies disappear from boxes and reappear from behind a curtain. I do not make doves or flowers pop out of a magic top hat—though I suppose I could. Rather, I am a magician of the old sort—quite uncommon in these days when so few people believe in *real* magic. In fact, my problem is that so few people do believe in magicians like me—or in the King I serve."

Jodi and Martin heard a note of sadness in his voice and caught a glimmer of deep unhappiness in his eyes. "What kind of magic do you do?" Jodi asked as she sat on the floor.

"Well, take my friend here," Waymond said, patting the yellow-brown head of an enormous cougar that appeared beside him without so much as a drum roll or burst of smoke. The cougar began to purr and bathe Waymond's hand with a great broad tongue. "His name is Reginald, and he's a friend of mine. He's from that special place I mentioned where your help is desperately needed."

Jodi and Martin's mouths had opened slightly when the cat had appeared. Now, they closed them and frowned as skeptically as they could. "All right," Jodi asked, trying to laugh, "what's the trick?"

The cougar growled slightly down inside his throat and put one wide paw up on the screen, nearly pushing it in. Through the fine mesh came the tips of five rather enormous claws. Jodi quickly scooted backward. When Martin saw that she was afraid, he decided it was up to him to make the illusion disappear. He pushed on one of the cougar's claws.

"Ouch! It's real!" he cried, turning to Jodi for an explanation.

"Nonsense," she stated, trying to sound as if she knew all about cougars that appeared from nowhere. She went to the screen and stared out at the beast beside the stranger. She could see the wind ruffling the cougar's fur; she could smell an earthy smell on his upheld paw; and she could definitely hear his deep purr-rr-rr vibrating drowsily through the air. She trembled and withdrew. "Ohhh," she said quietly, looking at Waymond. "He's your friend?"

"Back inside," the magician told the cougar.

"Right," said the cat and disappeared with a yawn.

A Knock on the Door

Waymond sat crosslegged on the porch, looking in at the children. "Now, about your question: Yes, he's my friend. And he and some good children much like you need our help! You see, those children, the Land from which I came, and the animals of that Land are all in great danger. You two are needed to be part of the rescue expedition."

"But . . . but why don't you just call the police? Or the army?" Jodi asked, feeling very confused and in need of a simple way to say no.

The magician laughed. "In the Land from which I come, there are no police or army—except children like you who are both brave and good."

"But why'd you pick *us*?" Jodi asked, tilting her head to one side. "We're not brave."

"You two were chosen because you try to be good children and can *believe*," Waymond said patiently. "You, Jodi, notice when animals and people are sad or hurt, and you would love to be bold enough to help them. You even believe your stuffed animals hurt when you accidentally drop them, and you used to cry as you bandaged them. You, Martin, believe the heroes and villains you see in cartoons and movies are real and really do fight for good and bad things. I know you very much would like to be one of the heroes . . . if only you had the chance. But, most of all, you two were chosen because you have love in your hearts."

Jodi looked with wonder at her brother, nodded, then turned back to the magician. "Gosh," she softly said, "I wish our mom and stepfather thought of us that way."

Waymond smiled, and the tip of his long beard rose. "They do, though they may not always act as if they do. But, on the other hand, you two may not always have the courage to let people like your parents know how much you really love them! If you will answer the call I bring you, I promise that you will be strengthened so that everyone—especially your parents—will be able to *see* how much you love and care for them."

"Hmm," Jodi murmured, half convinced. "What exactly is it you need us to do?"

Waymond nodded, pleased by her question. "I need Martin's belief in the good guys and the bad because the Land that Reginald and I are from is threatened by one of the worst bad guys ever. And Jodi, I need your feelings of love and tenderness for both animals and people, because we must free some children who have been captured and must help the animals who are being threatened. The three of us—and more friends I'll not name just now—must stop this bad guy, as Martin would call him, and his army of slaves. Otherwise, a lot of children and animals, as well as the Land itself, are going to suffer more than I can tell you." His brown eyes looked very serious as he stared through the screen at them.

"Who is this bad guy?" Jodi asked, scooting closer to the window.

Waymond turned his head left and right, peering cautiously up and down the street. Leaning toward Jodi, he quietly said, "Names have great power, and to name him would be to call him to us. So, for now, I can only say that he is the Magician's Bane. I am the magician involved, and this bad guy could well be the bane of my existence."

For a moment a hush spread over the neighborhood; car sounds ceased, and the birds stopped singing. Even the wind held still. Jodi turned to Martin, who sat wide-eyed beside her, and whispered, "A bane is something deadly, like a poison."

"Ahh," Waymond sighed, leaning closer to the

screen, "this bane is more than that. *This* bane is a sorcerer who brings ruin and woe—to children like you and to the Land of the King I serve."

Chills raced suddenly over Jodi and Martin, and they drew back. Then Jodi's forehead wrinkled with a slight frown. "Who is this king you keep mentioning?"

Waymond sat back with a broad smile. "For now, I'll tell you only that he is both very loving and very powerful. But though he is very powerful, he depends on people like you and me to be . . . well, sort of pipelines for his power."

"How can we be . . .?" Martin began, but Jodi cut him off.

"No!" she practically shouted, feeling a sudden attack of fear. "We couldn't leave the house."

"Oh, snail snares and tortoise traps!" the magician said. "You both have your parents' permission to go as long as you tell them where, approximately, you're going and when, approximately, you'll be back. In fact, if they knew how much this adventure could strengthen you, they'd encourage you to go. I will admit, however, that they might think me rather strange." He laughed gently as he looked in at them.

"At least tell us more about this king and the bane," Jodi insisted anxiously.

"I can say no more than I already have," Waymond stated, standing.

"Wait," Jodi said quickly. "What could *we do* about this bane?"

"Fox boxes and heron crates, Jodi! I've already told you," Waymond said with increasing impatience. He sighed. "I need your love for other children and for all endangered and mistreated creatures. And I need your desire to be brave."

"*I* want to be brave, too," Martin said stoutly.

"I know you do," Waymond said with a gentle smile. "And I'm offering you just that opportunity: to do something *really* brave, *really* good. Furthermore, it's not something you'll do just to please someone for a while. No, if you do what the King and I ask—and it will not be at all easy, mind you!—you will be remembered for quite some time."

Jodi and Martin stared at each other. The Monopoly game was forgotten. Their fears and shyness were forgotten. The fact that supper was less than an hour away was forgotten. Jodi bent down to look out at Waymond again. "You can't tell us any more about what we're going to be expected to do?"

"You're to be yourselves, nothing more."

"What about Mom and Richard—won't they be worried?"

"I'll leave them a note," Waymond said with a wink of one twinkling brown eye.

"What'll you say?" Jodi asked.

"Go read it," the magician suggested, pointing toward the fireplace mantel. There, a large sheet of brown paper hung on a ruby-headed pin.

Martin and Jodi went quickly to read the tall, purple letters:

HAVE GONE ON A HUGE ADVENTURE WITH A MAGICIAN. WILL BE BACK AS SOON AS POSSIBLE. <u>PLEASE</u> DO NOT WORRY! LOVE, Jodi & Martin

Excitement burst within the two children. They ran back to the window. Jodi cried, "Can I take Benji with me?"

With a sparkle in his eyes, Waymond said, "You may take as many of your stuffed animals, clothes, socks, and other things as you are willing to carry." He lifted one finger in caution. "I must warn you, however, that the way will be long and difficult. You may grow tired of carrying too heavy a load."

"How long will we be gone?" Jodi inquired.

"I can't say; possibly only a day or two, possibly a very long time—or possibly only the time it takes an eye to blink." He winked.

Jodi and Martin ran to their bedrooms. Socks and clothes and toothbrushes and various things all flew into their packs, along with a blanket for each. And in between his spare shirt and clean underwear, Martin laid a toy sword—just in case one wasn't provided. In minutes, they were ready to begin.

Chapter 2

Along the Creek and Beyond

*J*odi and Martin started off as though the adventure were nothing more than a brief holiday or a trip to the park. Martin even thought of a friend who might like to come along. He didn't know that magicians are choosy of their company.

"Can I go ask our friend Eric if he wants to come?" Martin asked brightly, lengthening his steps to keep up with the magician.

As Waymond hurried them down the shady side of Mulberry Street, he looked at Martin. "Is he a good boy who *really* wants to be brave?"

"I think so," Martin replied, glancing at Jodi for support. "He stood up to some kids who called him a sissy 'cause he wouldn't throw rocks at the school windows." Martin grinned as he added, "And he was brave enough to ask that bully, Max Fredricks, to come with us to Sunday school."

Waymond laughed in a musical way that sounded like a wind chime. "Ah, that *is* bravery. But would he be brave enough to fight Murks?"

Martin and Jodi stopped suddenly. "Murks?" Martin asked in a small voice. "What are they?"

"Shadow dwellers," Waymond explained.

"Are they dangerous?" Jodi inquired.

"Only at night and only to those who are afraid," the magician said. He began walking quickly down the street, swinging his carpetbag.

"Oh," Jodi muttered uncertainly, hurrying on behind Waymond. Martin followed reluctantly.

"What about Eric?" he asked the striding magician. "Where does he live?"

"Around the next corner and up the block," Martin answered, his mood lightened by the prospect of taking an older friend along.

Waymond stopped and rested his fists on his hips. "Well, you may ask him. I'll wait here."

Jodi and Martin turned the corner to go toward Eric's house. When they looked back, the magician had vanished. They blinked, wondering if they had been dreaming the whole time.

However, when they joined Eric in his living room, they learned that he certainly did not think they had been dreaming. In fact, he practically whooped, "Waymond? Waymond's come for you, too?" Eric's green, yellow-flecked eyes fairly sparkled in his squarish face.

"Yes," Jodi said, surprised. "You mean you know him?"

"Of course. Lots of kids—well, not so many—know Waymond."

"He didn't say he knew you," Jodi challenged. "He asked if you were the sort who really wanted to be brave and could fight Murks—whatever they are."

"Oh, he knows what I can do," Eric laughed. The blond-haired, athletic-looking boy ran off to pack and roll up his blanket. "Just a minute," he called from his room.

"Where're you off to now?" the voice of Eric's mother came.

"Martin, Jodi, and I are going up the creek," Eric explained. He returned carrying his pack and grabbed some cold biscuits from the kitchen. He put the biscuits into his pack as he rejoined Jodi and Martin.

"Well, be careful," his mother's voice warned. "Watch cars when you cross the streets, and stay out of the water! I don't want your feet wet; you know how easily you catch a cold." The voice followed Eric as he and the Westphall children went out the front door; it continued to follow him as the trio walked across the front yard: "And do be careful if you go to the clubhouse; don't step on nails, especially rusted ones, and watch falling off the edge. . . ."

Waymond was waiting for them at the street corner. "Hullo, Ric," he said, brightening. "Didn't know it was you Martin and Jodi went for, else I'd have come too—though I don't suppose it would have been a good idea to let your mother see me, not after last time."

"Last time?" both Jodi and Martin asked.

Eric and Waymond shrugged. They set off at a fast pace, and Jodi and Martin hurried to keep up. Eric, or Ric, told them, "It was only a small matter." He looked up at Waymond. "What is it this time—an epidemic of sleeping sickness or something?"

Waymond shook his head gravely as he strode on. "Much worse."

Eric began to frown. "Sneaks have gotten in and started a grass fire?"

"Close, but worse still," came the reply.

Eric frowned deeper and shook his head once. "Robbers? Have robbers pillaged Wayshead?"

For a moment Waymond stopped; the children noticed that his eyes had become dark. "Close again, but still worse, I'm afraid."

28

"Murks?" Eric asked, growing angry.

"Yes, and more," Waymond said, walking on. Then, in a tone so low that not even an eavesdropping squirrel could have overhead, the magician added, "And the Bane leads them."

By this time Jodi and Martin were not at all glad they had come with the strange magician, even if their friend did know him. In fact, they both were silently wishing they had never left their house. By now, spending the afternoon bent over the Monopoly game seemed a much better activity than any adventure with a stranger. Waymond seemed to read their thoughts.

"Cheer up!" he chuckled. "I've still got my bag," he patted it, "and my staff," he shook it. "So we'll be all right . . . if you've the courage and good sense I believe you have."

As Jodi and Martin exchanged unsure looks, Martin stumbled. "But . . .," he began, trying to catch up with the striding magician and Eric, "but what are. . ." Both Eric and Waymond shot him silencing glances.

Waymond frowned. "We've said enough for now."

They came to a bridge over a creek, and down into the creek channel Waymond ran. He stopped near the trickle of water in the paved bottom. He waited for the children, then set off at a rapid pace.

"Waymond," Eric began, glancing around at the backs of the houses on either side of the creek, "is the King in the Land?"

"Wherever he's most needed, that's where the King will be," Waymond stated. "In any case, he's depending on *us* to handle the rescue and the fighting . . . with his help, of course."

Jodi and Martin hurried along in the rear, trying to

hear each word that was said, as well as trying to keep their feet out of the water and away from cans, broken bottles, old tires, and other trash.

"Rescue? What rescue?" Martin asked. "And what fighting?"

"Oh," Waymond replied, trying to be casual, "some children have been captured—and they weren't even Zooks! We may have to do battle to free them."

"Zooks? What are Zooks!?" Martin—who was becoming frustrated as well as puzzled—practically cried. "I don't under . . ."

"You'll understand everything," Waymond winked, "at the proper time."

Jodi timidly tugged on Eric's shirt. "But what *are* Zooks?" she whispered.

Eric glanced at her as he continued to march ahead. "When called, we Zooks fight for the King."

"But I've never heard of Zooks," Jodi said, blinking with a blank expression.

"That's because you've never been called," Waymond explained, "until now."

"Are we Zooks now?" Martin inquired, hoping he was because it sounded super to fight for a king when called upon.

"Not officially," Eric said. "Until you've met the test, you're only apprentice Zooks."

"You never told me about them," Martin protested, kicking a can.

"Part of the Ceremony is that we're sort of sworn to silence," Eric said seriously. "We're supposed to *act* like Zooks, not *talk* about them."

"What ceremony?" Martin sighed.

"*The* Ceremony . . . the Ceremony of the Upraised Swords," Eric replied, walking faster to keep up with Waymond. "You'll see . . . maybe."

They travelled in silence until they passed near the

boys' clubhouse. It was built in an old oak tree near the creek. A thin, black-haired boy was playing on the lower platform.

"There's that boy who came to live with old Mrs. Harkess," Jodi noted sadly. "Did you hear that his parents were killed in a car wreck, and he lost his speech because of it?"

Eric and Martin, however, were more concerned about protecting their clubhouse than about the quiet, poorly dressed boy. Eric yelled, "Get down. Get away from there!"

The boy did not move a muscle; instead, he stared at Eric with large, dark eyes. Eric and Martin would have gone and made him get away from the clubhouse, but Waymond urgently beckoned to them.

They walked on, down in the creek bed where no one noticed them, through the town for a mile or more. Passing fewer and fewer houses, they came at last to the outskirts of the town. Open fields began to appear on either side. The creek's bottom and sides no longer were paved, and in places walking was difficult because of muddy pools. Weeds grew tall near the boggy spots, forcing the quartet to weave left and right. Frequently they had to jump the meandering thread of water, which was coming from the farmlands beyond.

As they walked, Jodi thought about all the magician had said. When they were well away from houses, she worked up her courage to ask, "Mr. Waymond, can you tell us more about this Magician's Bane?"

Waymond stopped and produced a bluejay-bright handkerchief from thin air. Jodi blinked in surprise. Waymond lifted his long beard with one hand and wiped his throat with the cloth. "Wait a while," he said, going on. The kerchief disappeared as easily as it had come.

He climbed up the creek bank and turned to help

the others scramble out. When they all were beside him he strode to the top of a long, low ridge. With one hand shading his eyes from the setting sun, he surveyed the farmlands. "Our path appears safe for now," he announced, "so we can talk more freely." He led them down the ridge and out across the golden-lit, brown fields.

Walking beside Waymond, Jodi asked, "Will *we* have to fight the Bane?"

He neither turned nor slowed. "I sincerely hope that only I will ever face *him*, and that you will have to deal only with the lesser creatures of his making."

"Such as Murks?" Martin asked.

"And maybe a Wrath or two," Waymond answered.

"Don't we need swords or something?" Martin asked breathlessly.

"You may get one—if the proper time comes," Waymond replied.

"A real sword?"

"Very real," Waymond said in a low voice, turning.

"Great!" Martin exclaimed, stumbling behind Waymond over the plowed field.

All this time, Eric had been silent. Martin dropped back to walk beside him and looked at his serious face. "Have you used a real sword before?" he asked quietly.

"I . . . I had one," Eric said so Waymond could not hear.

The sun set. The air became cooler and cooler as blue-purple darkness stole into the sky behind the fading sunlight. Hunger made Jodi's and Martin's stomachs squirm and growl, and they gobbled down the biscuits Eric had brought. The biscuits, however, were not nearly enough. To make matters worse, their feet began to ache from walking on the rough ground.

Waymond kept on at a steady pace, leading them toward a wandering line of trees. The trees were tall and ominously dark. Seeing the trees, Eric quietly said, "There's the boundary. The Land is just beyond the River."

Boundary? Land? Jodi and Martin looked at each other quizzically. They both had visited this river before, and it had always looked like any other ancient river. Only a few weeks earlier, Martin and his stepfather had spent a dismal, luckless afternoon fishing along its banks, and his stepfather had said nothing about a "land" on the opposite shore.

But Jodi and Martin were too tired to ask for an explanation. They shivered from a chill as they looked toward the barrier of trees. They smelled a thick, watery scent and heard a distant rushing of water. How would they get across, they wondered, and what would they find on the other side?

Looking at each other, sharing the same weariness and fear, they almost asked Waymond if they could go home to food and comfort. But Jodi resolutely tightened her lips and took Martin's hand. "Nothing ventured," she remembered her mother saying, "nothing gained."

Darkness settled over the farmlands as the four travellers climbed through a barbed wire fence and walked in single file toward the black wall of trees. The land became so dark that Jodi and Martin completely lost their bearings; for all they could tell, north might have become south.

Waymond, however, continued to stride forward. Perhaps, Jodi thought, magicians can see in the dark. She could not, and more than once she stumbled over a rock. "Please, sir," she asked at last, "could we have a light? My toes are getting bruised."

Waymond stopped, blinking at her as though waking. "Why, of course! How negligent of me to forget that the King sent each of you a gift—your first from him. What sort of light would you like?"

"A bright flashlight!" Martin said at once.

"A candle would do very well," Jodi said, reasoning that a small light would be less likely to attract any wild beasts lurking about.

Eric said nothing and kept his eyes on the trees ahead of them.

Waymond set his carpetbag on the ground and opened it. Both Jodi and Martin leaned over to peer into the bag, but neither could see a thing inside it. From it Waymond first pulled a long flashlight, which he gave to Martin, then a tall candlestick with an already lighted candle, which he gave to Jodi.

"Thank you!" Jodi exclaimed, surprised that the candle flame did not waver or give off heat.

"Wow!" Martin cried as he switched on the flashlight and shined it over the rolling land that sloped down to the trees.

"Those lights—because they are from the King—are very important. Do not lose them," Waymond cautioned sternly.

"We won't," Jodi assured him.

"Eric, don't you want a flashlight?" Martin asked his friend.

Eric slowly turned. "What?"

"I asked, don't you want a light too?"

"Naw," Eric said quickly. "But they are useful against Murks."

Hastily Martin shined his light over the ground. "Are they here?"

Eric looked at the ground near Martin's feet. "You could be standing in one."

Martin jumped back. "Where?" he demanded.

Eric pointed to a pool of especially dark darkness

34

lying in a slight hollow of the ground. It was a puddle of darkness much like those which lie under beds at night and make children afraid to step out of bed after the lights are turned off.

"Right there," Eric said, turning toward the river. "And there," he pointed, "and there also."

Jodi held her candle toward the pools of shadow. "I don't see anything but nighttime."

"I doubt if Murks have crossed the River," Waymond told Eric, then turned to Jodi. "Besides, none of us is very much afraid yet."

"Ohh," Jodi breathed, becoming as still as a tree.

Eric, meanwhile, was walking slowly toward the river, apparently lost in thought. "Waymond," he said quietly without turning his head, "I hear laughter. Are Stenches at the boundary too?" There was a nervous edge in his voice.

"Yes, it sounds like them," Waymond replied, snapping shut his bag. Both Jodi and Martin jumped when they heard the sharp sound. "They're probably standing guard." He tilted his head and peered at Eric. "Say, Zook lieutenant, you're not afraid, are you?"

"No," Eric quickly answered. "It's just that . . . well . . . nothing." Rapidly, he walked on.

Waymond and the Westphall children resumed their march toward the trees. In a halting voice Jodi asked, "Mr. Waymond, how come we've never heard of the land or seen Stenches or Murks when we walked along the river?"

Without missing a step, Waymond turned his head and replied, "Only those who are called or sent by the King can enter the Land . . . or even see across the boundary into it. As for Murks and Stenches, you probably *have* seen them but didn't know what they were."

Jodi, although still confused, decided to drop the matter—at least for the time being.

Martin tugged on the magician's left sleeve and asked, "Won't the Stenches try to keep us from crossing the river?"

"Oh, don't worry about Stenches; they just smell bad," Waymond said, wrinkling his rather long nose. "People don't usually go where there's a bad smell, so Stenches make fairly good guards. But they're harmless."

"Are we likely to meet worse things than Stenches and Murks when we cross?" Jodi asked, shielding her candlelight with one hand so she could see clearly past it.

"Worse . . . or better," Waymond replied, shifting his bag from one hand to the other. "The Land of the King contains many things; among them is a place where we can get a good night's rest. You'll need it, because we have a long way to go tomorrow."

"How far?" Martin yawned, holding his flashlight against his chest.

"Um, about a jay's flight across the prairie and—if you're not too tired by then—a coonet's run through the Forest."

"Coonet?" Jodi asked. "What's that?"

"You'll see. They're quite friendly . . . sometimes *too* friendly!" Waymond laughed a musical laugh and led them down a winding ravine toward the river.

They wound down until they came among a thick grove of willows. There the laughter Eric had heard became louder. It was almost like the sound of water sliding by, but it also had the strange quality of branches scratching and unseen things rustling. It was a mixture of many things that when alone in a forest one cannot exactly identify. One might have been tempted to ignore the sounds as being nothing

. . . but to Jodi and Martin the laughter was full of quiet threats.

"Are you *sure* Stenches are harmless?" Jodi asked, feeling goose-bumps rise as the bubbling-rustling laughter came from nearby willow thickets.

"I should say so!" Waymond laughed loudly. At once the sounds stopped. "They know we bring light and laughter!"

When his voice ceased, the sounds started— creaking, moaning, dry rubbing. Jodi shivered and held her candlelight toward some of the noises. They faded. She felt comforted and hurried to catch the others.

They had gone to the water's edge and were looking up and down the river. Jodi and Martin stood behind Waymond as he peered into the darkness and whistled shrilly. Before them, the river ran with untold breadth and depth. Its waters sounded heavy and powerful.

"Now where has the ferryman got off to?" the magician wondered. "Oh well, guess we'll have to use our own boat."

He set his carpetbag on the ground and opened it. Rubbing his long-fingered hands together, he peered into the darkness inside. Martin could not resist the temptation to use his flashlight. He shined it right inside the bag. Sure enough, it seemed empty!

"Did you have to do that?" Eric asked with sharp annoyance.

Martin, chastised, switched off his light.

Waymond reached down into the bag; almost all of both his arms disappeared into it. He grappled with something big and heavy and pulled it out with difficulty. It appeared to be a bundle of rubber sheets. He set the bundle on the riverbank and pulled a cord attached to it.

With a whoosh, air began rushing into the bundle, expanding it. In seconds, a rubber raft lay before them, complete with two paddles. Waymond and Eric launched the boat and held it to the shore. Waymond motioned for Martin and Jodi to step into it. It bobbed on the water's surface as they climbed in. Eric and Waymond then climbed in too. They each took a paddle and pushed the boat away from the bank.

As the light craft drifted out into the darkly flowing current, Jodi felt real fear; now, for the first time, she realized that they were entering the Great Unknown, leaving home and safety far behind.

She watched Eric and the magician silently sinking their paddles into the dark water, forcing the boat forward. Then she tried to see past them. Darkness lay heavily upon the water, and a foul odor drifted across it. She held her nose and snorted, "Phew!"

"Stenches," Eric commented without breaking the rhythm of his paddling.

"Even on the water?" Martin asked. Fearfully he looked around and down at the water swirling against the sides of the raft.

"Yes," Eric answered. "They can go just about anywhere—but they don't like to go where flowers are blooming. They *hate* the smell of flowers."

"The Stenches stink like that dead mouse we found," Martin said.

"Or like those old eggs you broke," Eric added.

The smell grew worse as they neared the far bank. There it rose up like a fog. Cold it was, and heavy, with a nastiness such as Jodi imagined would come from an old coffin being opened. And with the smell came chilling laughter. Empty voices darted at them, snickering in a way that raised chills on Jodi and Martin; they cowered in the boat, knowing that alone they never could have crossed the river. Waymond

and Eric, however, stroked steadily on, breathing as little as possible.

When they reached the other shore, the foul smell and mocking laughter began to fade. As Waymond drew the raft against the bank and let the children jump out, the stink drifted away. Jodi felt as if they had passed through an evil barrier. "We made it," she whispered, shielding her candle as she looked back across the sullen, swirling water.

"Too bad he didn't," Eric said quietly, pointing.

Jodi turned, looked, and screamed—holding her hands to her mouth.

Chapter 3

Murks Arise

*W*aymond scrambled along the muddy bank. A dozen feet away, his legs in the water, lay a man whose face probably had once been quite pleasant. Now, he lay spread on the mud—quite dead.

"It's Wharford, the ferryman," Waymond explained, dragging the body up the bank. As the children watched in horror, Waymond disappeared into the woods with the corpse. Yellow lightning flashed through the darkness, startling the trio of watchers. Then the magician reappeared. As he stood above them cleaning his still glowing staff, they could see tears on his cheeks. "Poor Wharford," he muttered. He shook his head and slid down the embankment to the raft.

Eric shouldered his pack and climbed atop the riverbank. "Now, the Murks are guardians," he said quietly, staring toward the woods.

"Are they what killed . . .?" Jodi began.

A sharp hiss of air startled her as Waymond deflated the raft. Carefully he folded it and stuffed it into his bag. Wiping his hands on a kerchief, he said, "Let's hurry away from here."

Eric led the way, turning his head left and right. Jodi thought he had changed since they crossed the river; now he seemed to be a hunter and walked warily, like a cat outside at night. She watched him sniff and stare here and there, his eyes probing the black spaces among the over-watching trees. She noticed that Waymond, too, was observing Eric; but the magician was frowning as though he thought something was amiss with the boy. However, he said nothing, and Jodi decided Waymond's frown was caused by the ferryman's death. She closed her eyes and shook her head, trying to clear from her memory the image of the dead man.

As they walked on, Jodi listened. Except for the laughter of the Stenches behind them, all was silent. And, as they went further into the bottomland of moss-draped, ancient trees, the silence grew ever deeper around them.

"It's so quiet," she whispered. Even her whisper seemed loud.

"Shhh," Eric cautioned.

"But won't talking keep the Murks away?" Jodi asked softly.

"No, 'cause they'll hear the fear in your voice," Eric replied, "and fear brings Murks."

Jodi and Martin each swallowed hard, their eyes wide open as they strained to see into the darkness beyond Jodi's candle flame. Thoughts of the dead ferryman came to them, and they wished they could return to the safety of their home. As it was, however, they tried to master their fear as they walked stealthily in file between Eric and Waymond.

They meandered through the bottomland forest for almost an hour. Closer and closer the trees and darkness gathered about them until Jodi felt as though she were groping through a giant's pocket. At last, they came to the edge of the throng of mossy trees. Jodi and Martin breathed sighs of relief. She glanced back at the thick darkness, glad to be free of it, then looked ahead. A hill rose before them—a dark shape looming above the level of the forest. It was bulky against the blue-blackness of the starry sky.

"That's Fearinmont," Waymond said, pointing to the hill with his staff as he went ahead of Eric. "Before the invasion, boundary wardens were stationed on it. We'll camp there."

Tiredly, the children followed him up a winding trail to the hilltop. As they trudged upward they glanced at the deep shadows that lay all about in hollows on the hill's bare sides, and Jodi wondered grimly what had happened to the boundary wardens. But, despite the ominous shadows and gloomy thoughts, Jodi's and Martin's spirits were brightened by the cool, fresh air blowing over the hill. The breeze was a great relief after the dank, silent atmosphere of the bottomlands.

"It surely feels good to be out of the forest," Jodi said, removing her pack as they stopped atop the hill. She looked down at the bottomland, then out over the treetops and around. Slowly, she turned in a circle. To the east and south ran the dark, wandering curve of the trees along either side of the river. To the west and south, starlight shone silvery on rolling grasslands.

Breathing deeply, Jodi looked skyward. There, stars were twinkling points of light behind a thin haze of clouds, which was being pushed southward by the breeze. Strangely, the cloud haze stopped at the river and seemed to flow out in circular patterns. Figure it out, she could not. But she stopped wondering about it because the breeze felt thoroughly delicious upon her cheeks and took her mind off all questions. She smiled, set her candlestick down, and began to unpack.

They ate food that did not need to be cooked, because Waymond thought it unwise to build a fire and draw attention to their location. Soon, they rolled up in their blankets to go to sleep. Despite the fact that Jodi and Martin were not used to sleeping on hard ground, tiredness closed their eyes almost immediately. They slept fitfully—until they felt something cold slinking over them.

Jodi woke suddenly with a chill. She blinked, wiped her eyes, and tried to see into the darkness. She looked for her candle, but it was no longer burning. As she groped around for it, her hand touched something that made her draw back in dread.

"Waymond!" she gasped, but her voice seemed smothered by the chilling shadows around her. Wildly, she looked toward Martin. He, too, was wide awake. He was staring speechlessly into the darkness. Waymond and Eric slept peacefully nearby, apparently undisturbed by the cold touch that had awakened Jodi and Martin. "Waymond!!" Jodi croaked, her throat tight with fear. *Why, oh why, didn't he awaken?*

With pounding heart she darted across the space separating her from Martin. They wrapped their arms around each other as they did at home when one of them woke from a bad dream. Slowly, the chill withdrew.

"What is it?" Martin asked. "And why don't Eric and Waymond wake up?"

"Maybe . . . maybe they're like the ferryman," Jodi whispered.

Martin gasped, wide-eyed. "You mean they might be d . . .?" The thought of being left alone in a strange place far from home with two dead friends made him shiver against Jodi and begin to cry.

"Your flashlight . . . where is it?" Jodi asked with sudden strength.

Martin felt around on the ground by his blanket. However, his hand sank into a pool of freezing darkness, and he withdrew it with a shriek. "It's all around us!" he whispered, almost wild with fright.

For several minutes they sat holding each other, staring into the night. As their fright grew less, they began to see the hilltop around them. It ran down curving slopes to the trees on two sides and to the grasslands on the other two sides. Above, the haze had been blown away, and the moon was rising in the east, thin and new.

"Is the chill gone?" Martin's voice trembled.

Jodi mustered her courage and put one hand out beyond the blanket. At first it met nothing. She reached further, then further still until she grasped her candlestick. At the same moment, a heavy, cold shadow wrapped itself around her arm! She cried out and jerked back her arm. Clutching the candlestick, she groaned, "Please light . . . *please!*"

The flame atop the candle flickered into life; a dim glow spread around them. Instantly, the cold shadows withdrew with faint sighs. Emboldened, Jodi held up her flame. The shadows withdrew further, slinking back toward the edges of the hilltop. "Ha!" she almost shouted, "You *are* afraid of the light." She began to crawl forward.

As she went, the chilling blackness flowed away, sighing as it slipped down the hill toward the trees below. "Go on!" she commanded the shadows, standing to walk cautiously forward. The shadows withdrew even more, sinking down into a gloomy hollow of the hillside.

With sudden bravery, Jodi ran down Fearinmont to the hollow. She thrust the King's light into the shadowy space. A dank wind burst up and raced down the hill toward the darkness of the trees. Jodi nodded in triumph and returned to Martin. By then he had found his flashlight and was trying with trembling fingers to switch it on.

"Don't worry," Jodi said, "the Murk that was here has gone."

Martin finally managed to turn on the long, silver light. He aimed it down the hill and caught the shadow flowing toward the woods. Hit by the bright beam, the shadow flew into the gloom beneath the trees with a hiss of pain.

"So much for you, filthy Murk!" Martin said, grinning at his sister.

"I wonder if there are more of them about?" Jodi asked, frowning.

"We can't safely go back to sleep until we know," Martin said, holding his light down against his blanket.

"You're right," Jodi said grimly, taking Martin's hand as she stood. "Come on."

Reluctantly, Martin followed. "All right, Murks," he muttered, "where are you?"

He and his sister set off hand-in-hand around the hilltop. They passed the comfortably sleeping figures of Waymond and Eric and finished one circuit of the hilltop. Lower they went, making another round. Their lights shone here and there, poking into hollows, flashing behind rocks. Occasionally a shadow darted away, followed by a sighing hiss.

Climbing down a dozen or so feet, they circled the hill for the third time. Now, they came upon a deep cleft in the hillside. There lay a gloom much larger and thicker than any they had previously seen. It rose with an empty moan and resisted their lights.

"Hm!" Jodi snorted, squeezing Martin's hand when he began to back away. "A tough one." When Jodi squeezed his hand, Martin was reminded that he had courage of his own.

"Don't let it know we're afraid," he whispered, gripping her hand as he went forward with his powerful light shining into the huge Murk. "Shsst!" he hissed at it as you might hiss at a prowling cat.

Jodi came with him, holding her candle before her. The thick shadow quivered, and a foul-smelling breath enveloped them. As they kept on, the darkness gathered itself into the top of the cleft. Then, as Jodi and Martin boldly walked forward, the shadow leaped upward and raced down the hill trailing a sigh of pain.

Round and round the hill the children went, marching arm-in-arm. They whistled one of Waymond's happy tunes as they thrust their lights into nooks and crannies of Fearinmont, banishing several more gloomy shadows before they were satisfied that all the Murks had fled.

"Think we can sleep in peace now?" Martin asked, looking up at his sister's face softly lit in her candle's glow.

"At least they know we're no longer afraid. And I feel much better." She breathed deeply, looking up at the stars bright overhead and the moon slowly rising above them. "You know, it's pretty out here."

"Sure is," Martin agreed, looking at the stars. "Smells nice, too."

Jodi took another deep breath and began climbing back up the hill. She helped Martin scramble up one particularly steep part, then laughed as he came to

stand beside her. "I don't think we'd be much good as mountain climbers," she commented, brushing herself.

"Maybe not, but as Murk fighters, we're okay," he chuckled, going to his blanket.

Without another word they lay down, and soon they were sound asleep. This time their dreams were pleasant ones—of stars shining down and the new moon climbing high, of fragrant breezes and grasslands glimmering in silvery light.

Chapter 4

The Forest of Always

*W*hen the sun's friendly face rose over the eastern horizon the land for miles around first turned pink, then rose, and finally yellow. Mists lingering in the shallow valleys were lit silver-white before they burned away. Again, the quartet ate food that needed no cooking. Satisfied, they packed to continue their journey.

Quietly, but with a note of pride in her voice, Jodi told Waymond and Eric of the battle with the Murks the night before. The magician said only, "I'm glad you remembered to use your presents from the King."

"Are we likely to meet more Murks?" Jodi asked, keeping pace with Waymond as they went down the hill.

"Yes. They and their kind now roam the Land in great numbers."

"Where, by the way, are we?" Martin inquired.

Waymond's expression brightened; he spread his arms and turned in a circle as he walked, never once stumbling. Throwing back his face so the rising sun glinted within the brown curls of his beard, he laughed heartily as he completed his turnabout. "As I said, this is the Land of the King!"

"But isn't this just farmland?" Jodi asked uncertainly, looking around. It was then she noticed that nowhere in sight were farmhouses, barbed wire fences, or even cattle and horses grazing. And, as she looked skyward and in all directions, she saw no signs of human activity—no jet planes in the sky, no tractors plowing, no trucks running on highways. The land appeared quite empty. Jodi was instinctively frightened by the empty vastness of the land.

"See?" Waymond asked with a wink and broad smile. "You've left the land you know."

"We left when we crossed the River," Eric explained.

"Then . . . then where are we?" Jodi stammered in confusion.

Waymond lifted his eyebrows and let them fall, sighing once. "Frog gloves and hare hats! I've already told you; we're in the Land of the King!"

"And where's this forest you said we'd have to go through?"

Waymond led the way up a long, pale-green ridge. It curved back and forth to another hilltop. "The Forest lies spread in the middle of the kingdom—*the* Forest, that is . . . the Forest of Always. It's part of an ancient land and has always been here," Waymond said in a hushed voice. He winked and clapped Eric on one shoulder. "It and other lands and seas are just a step away, yet more than a step beyond . . . always close by, yet forever just out of sight—until danger threatens and someone must hearken."

"Are we . . . hearkening?" Martin asked, intrigued and excited.

"Most certainly we are," Waymond stated. "And the King will be *most* grateful—*if* we manage to carry out our tasks!"

"Who *is* this King?" Martin wondered, blinking sleepily.

"*The* King," said Waymond. He then began whistling a merry tune.

"What does he look like?" Jodi asked. "And what's he king of?"

"He is a very great King; many lands feel his love and justice, including this Land—which is very special to him. As for what he looks like, you'll have to be patient and see for yourself." Waymond was smiling hugely as he leaped a cattail-lined creek and held out one hand to help Jodi jump the trickling water.

As Martin sprang over the creek, he called, "I sure hope I get to meet this King; will he give me that real sword you mentioned?"

Waymond laughed pleasantly. "Maybe he will; many things are possible where he's concerned."

"Is he powerful?" Jodi asked, hurrying beside the magician.

Waymond's eyes lit up. "Most definitely so! In fact, he has the power of the very core of the universe at his command."

"Then how come he needs our help?" Jodi inquired skeptically. "Why doesn't he simply *zap* the . . . ?"

"Because that's just not the way he governs. He depends on humans—humans who believe in him—to do what needs to be done in the way of fighting . . . invaders. In that way, humans are strengthened and voluntarily become his servants— and friends."

"Excuse me, sir; I know I keep asking this . . . but how exactly are *we* supposed to help the King?" said Jodi, thinking of the awful look on the ferryman's face.

"We won't be helping the King," Waymond explained patiently. "We'll be helping the children, who I told you have been captured, and the Land and animals that are endangered. And you can help them—and indirectly help the King—by doing what your heart tells you to do."

That definitely was not the answer Jodi expected or wanted; she frowned and squinched up her mouth. "How will I know what my heart says?"

"By listening to it!" Waymond answered easily. He climbed the last few yards to the top of a hill and stopped to draw in a deep breath. He then aimed his staff toward the north. "There lies the Forest of Always," he announced.

The children clustered near him, eager to see their destination. Jodi and Martin looked where Waymond was pointing and saw a dark layer of green spreading over the northern horizon. Haze or smoke covered the middle part of it. In the center left they could dimly see a solitary mountain rearing its craggy peak above both trees and smoke.

"It's a long way away," Martin sighed, shaking his head doubtfully, "and my feet already are sore."

"They'll hurt more before we get there," Eric said. "Don't worry, though; you'll be toughened up by the time we're done with . . . with the Bane."

"I'm not sure I want to be toughened up," Jodi muttered, sitting down as she stared into the smoky distance. "And I certainly do not want to meet any Bane!"

"Nor do I," Waymond sighed, "but it is my task to do so." He pulled thoughtfully on his beard. "Your part of the mission, however, should be no more dangerous than dealing with his lesser servants—in much the same way you dealt with his Murks last night."

"Maybe the Bane's already left the Land," Jodi suggested hopefully.

"Nonsense," Eric snapped. "*He* would never voluntarily leave. Since his Murks were driven from the Land the last time, you can bet he's done nothing but plot how to erase his failure. There's no telling what creatures he's devised this time to do his bidding."

"Precisely so," Waymond agreed. "Now, on with it. Forward!"

They wound down the hill in single file. Waymond walked in front, swinging his staff like a drum major. His steps were light and long, and he whistled his merry melody into the clear morning air as though not a care existed. Martin tried to do the same but found that his whistle kept getting interrupted by worrisome thoughts.

Mile after mile of the beautiful land slowly passed underfoot. Around the travellers spread rolling, grassy hills. Occasionally, they saw a creek meandering among the hills; the banks of the ribbon creeks were bright with sprinklings of flowers. A few blossom-laden trees dotted the prairie with shade. And beneath the trees and the sprinkled flowers the turf of the plain was soft. Walking on the soft turf would have been a pleasure if their feet had not hurt.

They stopped for lunch at a tiny spring flowing from a hillside. The sparkling flow bubbled into a grass-edged bowl that headed a creek. White and yellow butterflies clustered like a fleet of bright-sailed, tiny boats around the bowl to sip the crystal water, even as the children knelt to do likewise. The water refreshed the travellers, and watching the butterflies relaxed them.

"Can we have a *real* supper tonight?" Martin asked, lying flat on his back. "With cooked food and maybe hot chocolate to drink?" A butterfly landed on the tip of his nose, and he crossed his eyes to look at it.

Waymond and the others laughed at Martin's comical expression, then the magician answered. "Tonight, we shall build a fire and cook a *real* supper. But, mind you," he added, "if we hear any strange noises we will have to douse the fire."

"You mean something may attack us during the night?" Martin asked as he sat up quickly. The butterfly flew from his nose in lazy circles.

"Possibly," Waymond admitted, looking skyward with a jerk.

Eric stood beside the spring, wiping water from his lips. Frowning, he pointed above his head. "Look, Waymond," he said in a low voice.

"I see it," the magician stated.

High, high up in the clear blue sky, a large shadowy shape drifted in a northward course above the prairie. Almost sullenly, like some great vulture, it flapped once and began to circle slower. In moments the shadow of dark wings and a broad body glided over the small group. The shadow chilled them like the coming of night. Frightened, Martin looked down; he caught his breath as he saw the spring darken and cease bubbling its happy tune. Jodi looked around and saw that the butterflies were hastily flying away in confusion.

"It's as I feared," Waymond announced. "The Bane's spies are out."

"What kind of spy is *that?*" Jodi asked, looking upward with the thought of finding a hiding place.

As though he had read her mind, Waymond said, "It's no good trying to hide out here in the grassland. That spy is one of the Wraths, and they have sharp eyesight. Gray eagles they were, from a mountain land far away where *he* dwelt long ago. But don't worry—the worst thing a Wrath can do, usually, is to shriek at you. That one will tell *him* we're coming, though. We shall have to change direction when it's gone."

They waited until the sullenly flapping silhouette of the Wrath climbed and sped out of sight to the north. Then Waymond pointed his staff westward. There they saw a creek meandering out of the dark green sea of trees of the Forest. "That's Apple Creek; we'll follow it to its source in the Forest on its western side. Along the Apple are rushes and willows that may screen us if any more spies appear." They packed up and wound their way down the hill.

They walked in silence for a long time as the wandering, sun-sparkled thread of the creek steadily drew nearer. Jodi, meanwhile, continued to worry. "Mr. Waymond," she finally asked, frowning. "What if Martin and I do meet *him?* What if you're not around to fight him, and we have to?"

Waymond gave her a grim look. "You must not become separated from me unless I leave you in a place that I have made safe! And if you should meet the Bane, you *must not* try to fight him yourselves, and you *must* remember your heart's desire."

"Which is?"

"Butterfly blinders! Have you forgotten already?"

"You mean," Jodi inquired, "my wish to be brave?"

"Yes," Waymond nodded. "So, if you do meet *him,* that is what you must do. Only then, you must do more than merely wish. You must do what your heart tells you—*no matter what happens!*"

Jodi saw in his look and heard in his voice a seriousness she had not before noted. She hurried to follow him to the creek, which curved gracefully back and forth toward the Forest.

At the mossy, cattail- and willow-cloaked edge of the water, Waymond paused and sniffed the air. The children sniffed too and immediately wrinkled their noses at a stink resembling that of sewers and rotting things.

"As I feared," the magician muttered to himself, "the invasion has spread. His Stenches have fouled even the Apple."

Jodi noticed that Waymond's eyes filled with tears as he surveyed the once lovely watercourse. Foul things floated down it, and the flowers and grasses along its banks were wilted and trampled. The smell and sight made Jodi turn away with a sickened feeling. "I'll bet it was pretty once," she observed.

Waymond nodded, waggling his beard. "And so it shall be again—if we succeed. However, matters are more serious than when I left. His slaves have been at work only a few days, but already they've done much harm."

The four friends walked along the fouled waters, holding their noses. Suffering in the stench of the clotted stream for an hour or so, their spirits became downcast. They began to feel dirty. When they could stand the feeling no longer, they returned to the prairie.

"It's like you said," Jodi told Waymond, keeping a watchful eye out for spies. "The Bane does bring ruin and sadness."

"Aye, he seeks to sap the very soul of life itself," the magician nodded sadly.

"*Could* he do that?" Jodi asked, frightened.

Waymond's eyes grew dark. "He has that power at his command—a power that, among us, only I could hope to resist."

"We may be stronger than you think," Martin declared, hurrying up beside his sister to take her hand; she looked at him skeptically.

Waymond gave the tired little boy a long, steady look. "I sincerely hope you are."

They walked on and on, up pale green hills and down across wide, shallow valleys. The land was rising all this time, climbing toward the vast plateau over which the Forest of Always spread its dark green blanket. By the time the sun was low in the sky, a breeze had sprung up from the west. It soon began bringing high and thin clouds to be set aflame by the sunset.

"Rain tomorrow, sure as the dawn," Waymond noted, pointing his staff toward the wispy, flaming clouds.

"I just hope we'll have a dry spot to sleep on," Martin complained. His legs ached fiercely, and he longed to lie down on a soft bed and sleep for hours. Only the hope of meeting the King and getting a real sword enabled him to keep up.

"We shall hope for no more than a *safe* place for our slumber," Waymond said. Jodi heard the grimness in his voice again.

"What will we do when we reach the Forest?" she asked, wishing she could soak her feet in the cooling waters of another spring.

"Scout around for news," Eric replied confidently. "Maybe the jays will know where the captive children are."

Waymond laughed. "Yes, they can't be kept in ignorance . . . if *he* hasn't blasted them."

"Oh, that's right," Eric said, thoughtfully. "Last time, he made a storm from the northern ocean blow all the birds away."

Waymond turned and went striding toward a rounded knoll perhaps a quarter mile away. Dried, brown grass streamed about his knees as he walked to the summit of the mound. Jodi was startled to see how well he and his brown clothes blended into the landscape. As he stood atop the small hill, he looked like a rugged tree outlined against the sunset. He soon motioned for the children to join him. Then, he pointed north with his staff. "There it is," he said simply.

Ahead, stretching to the horizon on either hand, lay an expanse of rumpled, very dark green treetops. Despite the westerly wind, they were not moving one bit. Great, deep shadows lay gathered under the skirts of foliage. A reek of smoke drifted over the scene like a shroud, and it was obvious that widespread burning was taking place in the depths of the Forest.

"Is the enemy cutting and burning the trees?" Eric asked anxiously as he pointed to several plumes of smoke. The smoke columns were rising slowly to join the general overcast that lay above the Forest.

"As rapidly as they can," Waymond muttered. Jodi noted that his rather broad lips became tightly clenched as though he were very determined about something. With a sudden laugh, he relaxed and flashed his eyes upon them. "But the Forest is great, and we have come in time—though only in the nick of time it would appear."

Beckoning to them, he led the children down the knoll and off at a fast pace toward the edge of the Forest. Martin sighed and shouldered his pack, wishing he had left his heavier belongings at home.

Twilight came rapidly. An eerie half-light settled in between the darkening ground and the hazy sky. The clouds thickened, sliding in from the west on a wind that had grown stormy. By the time the travellers reached the edge of the Forest, the wind was whistling through clumps of dead grass and sighing among the trees. Even in the dim light of dusk, they could see that the trees were much too large to be moved by anything less than a great storm. Like giant brown towers fifty or so feet from one another, the trunks reared above the dwarfed quartet. Branches spread and spread from the trunks like ribs of a roof for the world. Waymond and his band disappeared into the deep shadows that lay under the layers upon layers of leafy branches.

When they entered the Forest they also entered a heavy silence. High overhead they could hear the wind gusting through the treetops, but below—in the shadows—all was still. It was so still that Jodi noticed that she was having trouble breathing. She asked in a hushed voice, such as she would have used in a great cathedral, "Doesn't the air move down here?"

"Not much," Eric stated, looking around. Jodi noted that he again had become like a hunter or a wary cat stalking through a strange wilderness. Waymond, too, had begun to move more slowly, more cautiously. Jodi began watching her feet, being careful not to step on a stick and make a loud noise with its breaking. The silence absorbed them.

"Aaiieesskreecht!" burst an earsplitting wail from the trees overhead.

The children froze in terror. The petrifying wail was followed by a great flapping of wings. A form long and wide swooped down from the branches above. *"Aaiieeesskreecht!!"* it cried again, electrifying them.

Just before long talons gleaming in the dim light reached them, Waymond thrust up his staff. From its tip erupted a yellow blaze of lightning. The lightning scattered the shadows and illuminated a gray-feathered creature diving upon their heads. Blinded, the bird missed the children by inches and crashed heavily to the ground behind them. Waymond turned and levelled his staff at the bird as it lay stunned at the base of a giant tree. *Fffzzzuwff!* went jagged lightning from the staff's tip. *Whuuf!* the bird flamed and shrivelled in a ball of dense smoke.

While the smoke drifted away, the children slowly

recovered from the shock. Cautiously they went to see what remained of their attacker.

"Was it a Wrath?" Jodi asked, trembling as she walked behind Eric.

"Yes, but not anymore," Eric said, turning with a smile.

Jodi looked and saw an eagle, now of normal size. It sat against the base of the tree, blinking puzzled orange eyes at them from singed gray plumage.

"Oh, it's cute," Jodi said, going forward to examine it.

"Yes, now that the Bane's spell has been removed," Waymond said, coming up. "You can handle it; it's quite tame."

Jodi reached out one quivering hand and touched the bird's head. "It isn't even afraid of me," she murmured, wrapping her hands around it. "It just seems cold and frightened, like we are."

Waymond nodded, setting his staff tip in the ground. "Take it with you. Perhaps, since you're fond of animals, you can make a pet of it."

Jodi stroked the eagle's head, looking into its eyes as it blinked at her. "How could the Bane do evil things to harmless birds?"

Waymond raised one eyebrow and shook his head. "He can't tolerate beautiful or gentle things; nothing else so angers *him* . . . except love."

With the bird nestled under one arm, Jodi followed Waymond and the others deeper into the Forest. Thinking about what he had said, they kept their eyes on the lower branches, wondering what other monsters had been set loose within the Land. The silence once more enveloped them. And in it they soon began to hear the snickering, gurgling laughter of Stenches and the sighing of Murks.

Martin, stumbling along with one hand firmly gripping his sister's blouse, was nearly asleep when they came into a clearing. Waymond surveyed the area with a quick turnaround and nodded once as though in satisfaction. He lifted his staff high and stuck it into the ground in the center of the clearing. In a voice that carried far into the gloomy forest, he declared, "Here the staff and I shall spend the night, *come what may!*"

With that, he and Eric set about gathering firewood and building a conical stack of dry twigs and branches. Jodi sat on the ground near the staff and tried to comfort the gray, shaken eagle. Martin lay down with his head on Jodi's lap and went soundly to sleep. Soon, Waymond set the firewood ablaze, and in minutes steak and potato slices were sizzling in a skillet. Martin awoke, sniffing the frying food. He gazed hungrily at it and at the thick bread slices Eric had put on green sticks to toast near the flames.

Martin, rubbing his growling stomach, complained to Waymond, "If you can make a skillet and food appear, why can't you just zap up a finished meal?"

"Ahh," Waymond smiled, taking in a deep breath of the aroma of the cooking food, "half the fun—whether in building a fire or in cooking the food—is anticipation! Waiting for a blaze to lick its way up a well laid stack of firewood makes you appreciate the warmth once it reaches you, and the smell of cooking food . . . well, I can see by your drooling mouth how that makes you feel!"

"Speaking of anticipation," Jodi said, glancing toward the forest, dark-dark with its shadows shifting in the firelight, "I wish we knew what lies ahead for us."

"What lies ahead, Miss Jodi," Waymond said as his eyes sparkled, "is a good, hot meal—and hot chocolate!"

Fed and content, they unrolled their blankets by the

cheerful campfire. Waymond sat facing away from the blaze with his eyes wide open. Knowing that he was on guard, the children slipped into sleep.

During the long hours of darkness, only the magician and the eagle remained alert to the spies lurking around the clearing in the Forest of Always. And, strangely, the eagle, Waymond, and the spies all shared one thing: anticipation.

Chapter 5

A Day of Gloom

he dawn came slowly through grayness of mist and cloud. The children awoke and looked at the circlet of sky above the clearing. They could see thick clouds sliding past, snagging on the treetops. Fingers of mist poked downward into the shadowy, still Forest. Not a sound was to be heard.

"Good morning!" Waymond said with hearty cheerfulness. The children flinched and stared at him, then began to smile. He was beaming as he set about rekindling the fire and cooking their breakfast. "How about having ham and scrambled eggs and toasted muffins with butter running into them? Would that take the sadness of this gray day off your faces?"

"It would off mine," Eric said, rubbing his stomach.

"Mine too!" Martin echoed.

"I guess so," Jodi said grumpily; she was slow to wake up, having been bothered by troubling dreams late in the night—or at least she supposed the sights and sounds had been dreams.

"Sleep well?" Waymond asked, looking at Jodi as he set the skillet on the fire.

65

She shook her head. "Just before dawn I kept dreaming that I heard woodcutters felling trees, and I kept smelling the smoke of fires burning all around me. I woke up because I thought I was about to be dropped into one of the bonfires." She shuddered, wrapping her arms around herself. "I'm glad it was just a dream."

Waymond said nothing as he turned ham slices frying in the skillet.

"I woke up once," Eric told Jodi, "and did hear the sounds of woodcutters. They must work mainly late at night. Right, Waymond?"

"Yes," the magician replied. "Slashes, most likely."

"Slashes?" Martin inquired, pausing in the middle of a stretch and yawn. "What are they?" He was almost afraid to hear the answer.

"Slashes are some of *his* slaves—big, hairy things from deep mountain caves in the far north country. He's trained them to hate trees and use axes." Waymond smiled sadly through the smoke of their campfire and pointed to one edge of the clearing. "Over there is a spring where you can wash your faces. You may see Stench tracks around it, but don't worry; I've cleaned up the water." The children got washcloths from their packs and went to the spring.

Around the crystal eye of water they did in fact see many ugly, spidery tracks. Jodi shivered as she washed and hesitantly drank, then carried some water in a big, dried leaf back to her eagle. It gulped thirstily, throwing back its head to swallow. Its thirst quenched, the eagle looked gratefully at her.

After the children had eaten and packed their belongings, Waymond pulled his staff from the ground. "Onward!" he announced, swinging his staff around and around before shouldering it. Martin and Eric followed him, but Jodi hung back, looking at the campfire, which Waymond had extinguished. The magician stopped.

"What's wrong?" he asked gently.

She trembled slightly, and a tear slid down one cheek as she looked toward the dark, hazy woods. "I'm scared to leave here."

He immediately came back to her and put one arm around her shoulders. She leaned against him as he quietly said, "I know it's frightening to leave a small comfort you know is real to journey through uncertainty to a greater comfort you haven't seen. But believe me, no matter how much darkness lies ahead, the King's love will make the journey more than worthwhile. Besides, there's Wayshead," he concluded, starting off with her.

As they followed him down a broad, winding trail through the sea of mighty trees, Jodi regained control of herself and asked, "And what is Wayshead?"

"It's the Hall of the King," Waymond replied, patting her on the back with one hand as he swung his staff with his other hand. He smiled and looked ahead into the hazy woods. "It's a Hall such as I doubt you've ever seen—one of trees and ivy, flowers and meadow grass, and a silver-green river. All the animals love it because it is—or was—a place of great peace." His voice trailed off into sadness, but he set his jaw and lengthened his stride.

"Was?" Jodi asked, noticing that all the flowers around them on the forest floor hung limply on their stalks as though an early autumn had surprised them.

The magician answered, "I'm afraid that the Bane's slaves have destroyed it."

"And are we going there?" Martin asked, wishing the toy sword in his pack were real.

"I, at least, must," Waymond replied.

"What for?" Jodi inquired, frowning at the thought

that he might leave them somewhere while he went to the Hall.

"To see if either *he* or the captive children are there and to declare myself."

"What will we do while you go to Wayshead?" Jodi asked, her frown tightening.

"I'll leave you and Martin in a safe place," Waymond answered. He turned to look hard at Jodi. "And you must *not* leave that place—no matter what may happen!"

"Aren't we all going together on this mission?" Martin protested.

Waymond glanced at him. "We each have our own tasks," he said firmly.

That statement left the children with an empty feeling. In a suspicious tone, Jodi asked, "Didn't Eric say we were going to scout around for news from the jays?"

"Eric was speaking his thoughts, not mine," Waymond quietly noted. Then, with a light laugh, he added, "Besides, have you seen any jays?"

They gazed skyward, searching the tree branches with their looks, but not one sign of any bird or animal could they see.

"Perhaps at least one has remained," Eric said hopefully, holding one hand behind his right ear and listening carefully.

"Do you hear something?" Waymond asked, coming to a halt in the middle of the trail.

"No," Eric said after a moment. "I just thought I did."

They went on, winding back and forth along the broad, rutted trail. For a long while, the Forest on either side did not change. Its continual sameness made it hard to tell in what direction they were going, and the trees close around them made it hard to determine how far they had gone. Furthermore, since all the Forest seemed the same and the branches and clouds let no direct sunlight through, they could not have told if they were travelling in a circle or moving forward. The trail seemed to be going north, but occasionally it turned or dipped down to a slothful scummed creek or wound up to a bare knoll.

Suddenly, however, the Forest changed quite dramatically. Smoke came toward them, weaving gray fingers in and out among tree trunks. The smoke became thicker and thicker and rose higher until it seemed the group was walking in a fog. No ordinary fog it was either, for it leaped into their noses and throats, burning them. The children coughed dryly, and the eagle repeatedly sneezed.

"That's not just wood smoke," Eric noted, holding his chest as he coughed.

"No," Waymond agreed, wiping tears from his stinging eyes. "No ordinary fire could burn these trees, so he must have set *his* fire upon them. Smoke from that fire can be quite sickening."

In fact, they were becoming ill as they wended their way on through the hazy woods, trying not to breathe. Jodi began feeling dizzy, and Martin wished he could lie down and cry.

As tears blinded them they abruptly came out of the woods into a desolate clearing. No longer was there a Forest rising skyward. The trees had been attacked savagely, hewed and splintered until nothing was left but jagged stumps. Stumps and stumps and stumps beyond stumps met their tearful gazes. Among the stumps ran long, deep gashes in the earth where felled trees had been dragged away. The group wandered among the stumps, saddened by the hundreds of amputations. Sap oozed from the raw surfaces and gleamed in the gray light.

"Why didn't his slaves cut out the stumps too?" Jodi wondered, wiping her eyes again and again as tears ran freely down her cheeks.

"I imagine *he* thinks the Forest looks more ravaged this way," Waymond said grimly. He produced four blue handkerchiefs from the air, wet them from a bottle in his bag, and handed one to each child. "Hold those over your noses and breathe through the fabric. It will keep out the worst of the smoke."

Jodi and Martin gratefully wiped their eyes, squinting into the smoke, and rubbed some of the grime from their faces. They then held the bright cloths over their noses. The eagle, though, was unprotected; it continued to cough fitfully and flap its wings in discomfort.

After another mile or so they came to the first of many mounded fires they would encounter that dismal morning. The trunks of the trees had been dragged together and hoisted into a mountainous pile. The smoldering pile was casting off a reek of smoke like a huge smudge fire.

"Why is he destroying the Forest?" Jodi cried, drawing back from the tremendous heat of the burning.

"As I told you, he hates all beautiful things," Waymond replied. "Also, I think he needs the smoke to shut out the light and protect the imperfect eyes of his beasts."

"I'm glad they're not working now," Martin said quietly. "I'd hate to meet the beasts who are strong enough to chop down these trees and drag them together. Have you ever seen a Slash, Eric?"

Eric slowly shook his head, keeping his cloth held tightly over his nose and mouth. "No, and I hope I never do."

Mile after mile of slashed and burned Forest passed

as they plodded along. Each footstep stirred a puff of the ashes that lay thick upon the ground. Ash sifted down from the sky like a dry, evil rain. Soon, the travellers' hair and shoulders were coated with the gray flakes, making them look like very strange, old people. Their shoes were entirely blackened from the soot upon the earth, and they were sweating heavily from the heat of the burnings.

At times the trail disappeared under the scars where trees had been dragged or was blocked by limbs left lying about. Then, the forlorn group would have to wander around the mounds of charred tree trunks and glowing embers until Waymond could locate the trail again. It was a dreary, exhausting journey that seemed to have no end. On into the distance as far as they could see, the land was studded with the stumps of the hewn trees and darkened by the layer of smoke that reached up to mingle with the clouds.

At last, however, amid the grayness they saw a wall of dark green emerge ahead. A tongue of the Forest had been left, evidently the edge of where the Slashes had been working the night before. Beside the green wall lay felled trees, each much longer than a house, much thicker than the children were tall. Leaves hung limply from the arms, and white chips of wood lay scattered thickly around each stump. The scene was like the aftermath of a battle before the bodies are carried away. The quartet hurried among the felled giants and into the tongue of woods beyond. There, they stopped to rest near a "Y" branching of the trail.

The trees screened out much of the smoke, so the four took the cloths from their faces. "Ahhh," Waymond sighed, "air at last." With an effort, he smiled at his companions. "Let's eat."

No sooner had they sat down to eat lunch than Eric stood and cupped both hands behind his ears.

"What is it?" Martin asked, holding his sandwich in midair. "Slashes?"

"No," Eric whispered, turning a bit to his right. "A bird."

Waymond stood and whistled softly, beckoningly. In moments, a bright blue form flitted through the woods and circled over their heads.

"Rawww!" it cried down to them. "Here and there! Here and there! Rawwww!"

Waymond again whistled to the bird to show it that they were not *his* slaves, and the bird cautiously settled down to land on his outstretched finger.

"Rawww!" it said again, shaking its feathers to rid them of smoke and ashes. It stropped its beak on Waymond's finger and turned its head this way and that to peer at the children with shiny round eyes. "Raww," it murmured, preening its gray and blue feathers that were trimmed in black lines. It seemed happy to have found friendly beings.

Waymond, having given the bird time to rest, snapped his fingers before it. The bird sat up alertly. "Raw day . . . raw day in the Forest," it said with a shake of its feathers.

"What's the news, eyes of the air?" the magician asked.

"All bad . . . very all bad," the bird replied, turning its head up to peer at the smoke drifting through the trees.

"We've come to try to help," Waymond explained, sitting down. He put the bluejay on one knee and poured some water into a cup for it. The bird drank quickly, suspiciously eyeing the nearby eagle. Waymond continued, "We're going to try to rescue the children who refused to become Sneaks—if they still live."

"Live . . . live they do," the bird sang, looking cautiously about itself at the woods.

"Where?" Waymond asked. "At Wayshead or Crossingsend?"

"Neither nor . . . either or," the jay replied cryptically. "Could be . . . should be."

"You don't know for sure?" Waymond interpreted.

The jay shook its head several times and drank again from the cup. "Slashes, Slashes . . . fire and ashes; cut and burn . . . hate and spurn!"

"Yes, we know. But the children—where do you think they are?"

"Were here, now there . . . dragged and dragged, bound and gagged," the bird answered in singsong fashion, tilting its head from side to side.

"Poor children," Jodi softly said.

"It doesn't sound promising," Eric noted quietly.

The jay cocked its head and peered at the children. "Boy grim, girl fair, what're they doing there?" the bird inquired.

"They've come to help," Waymond replied. "Now, about the children?"

The jay shook its head, eyeing the woods again as though expecting something horrible to rush from it at any moment. "Lurk, lurk, darks of Murks . . . beasts come, beasts go, but where the good children are, I don't know." Then, with sudden fear, the bird flapped into the air. It circled once and cried "Rawww!" down at them as it flew into the smoke.

Waymond stood, brushing dirt off the seat of his pants. "At least we know the children are alive," he concluded.

"But are they at the Hall of Wayshead or at Crossingsend?" Eric asked, looking toward the "Y" branching of the trail.

Waymond sighed. "I don't know, but we must find

74

them. I myself will follow the left branch of the trail to Hopesmont. It rises above the Forest, and from its peak I can get a broad view of the Land. From Hopesmont I will go to Wayshead. Meanwhile Eric, you will follow the northward branch of the trail and investigate Crossingsend." He reached into his carpetbag and produced the hollow horn of some strange animal. The horn was long and curved and bound with wonderfully engraved silver bands. He presented the horn to Eric.

"This, as you know, is the Horn of Meet. Carry it with you as you use your Zook skills to spy out the deep caves of Crossingsend and discover if the children are hidden there. If you find them or hear news positive of their whereabouts, blow the horn to summon me and the Zooks." He looked gravely into the fourteen-year-old's eyes. "Be *very* careful not to let yourself be captured! As you know, the ways of the enemy are devious!"

Eric took the horn, slung its leather strap around his neck, and held it against his chest with both hands. "I'll be careful," he promised, smiling proudly. "You know how careful I can be."

Waymond nodded, looking at Eric in a puzzled sort of way—as though something obviously were amiss, something so obvious that he could not see it. But the magician was distracted by Jodi and Martin, who were clearing their throats and frowning anxiously. He smiled at them. "Don't worry, my friends; our separation will be only for a day—two at the most . . . if all goes well." He smiled again and laid his hands on their shoulders. "And don't worry about the fact that for now you don't seem to have a very important part in the mission; I am positive your roles will become clear to you before the final battle comes."

"The final battle?" Jodi cried, taking hold of

Waymond's sleeve. She looked at the darkening Forest where reeking smoke lingered and deep shadows lay in silence, then looked back at the magician. "Oh, please don't leave us!"

Waymond's face grew stern. "I must, but I will leave you in a protected place *until I return.*"

Still worried but silent, Jodi and Martin followed Waymond as he turned from the trail. He set off southwestward along the tongue of Forest that remained between slashed and burned plains of stumps.

They climbed over deadfalls and crawled under down-drooping vines. They meandered among giant tree trunks and came at last to the down-sloping edge of the vast plateau upon which the Forest lay. There, the earth was creased, and a creek ran from a spring at the head of the fold. Above the creek was a clearing; at the back edge of the clearing, near the wall of the Forest, stood a large, flat-topped boulder. It was covered with an ancient community of lichens. The children could tell that once the place had been beautiful, but now it was fouled by the work of Stenches and Slashes.

"Even Reeks have been here," Waymond said sadly, going into the clearing above the creek. Near the spring the magician turned slowly in a circle. "This," he explained, "is the head of the Apple. Once, it ran pure and bright . . . but as you can see, the enemy has trampled and scarred it and left refuse all about." With the tip of his staff he turned over several rusting food containers and pushed at a glittering mound of broken bottles. The trash littered both the ground and the creek, and the spring itself was muddied and trampled with the prints of huge, three-clawed feet. "Reek prints," Waymond said, pointing to the tracks. "The Reeks carry smoke from the fires and thrive on burning rubbish." Then, seeing that Jodi and Martin certainly did not like being left in such a place, he smiled. "Fear not, for the power given me by the King can make even this a haven."

He levelled his staff at the spring and trampled ground. Yellow lightning flowed forth, almost blinding the children. When they opened their eyes they saw that the clearing was bright with new grass and flowers, trash had been replaced by bright green moss, and pure water was gushing from among the glistening brown rocks of the spring. Jodi and Martin began to smile.

With the tip of his staff, Waymond carved a circle ten feet in diameter in the center of the clearing. He drew the line deep in the earth and made sure it was unbroken. The circle lay between the lichen-covered boulder and the spring. He beckoned to Jodi and Martin. Jodi let the gray eagle fly off into the trees near the clearing as she followed her brother into the circle. When they stood within it, Waymond raised his staff skyward. There, gray clouds flowed past toward the southwest, rumbling as though preparing for a long, heavy rain.

"Here let the King's power stand! Here let all evil be banned!" he cried upward. As his incantation ended, thunder crashed sharply from within the dark, hurrying clouds. Waymond smiled and looked at the children. "You see? We haven't been abandoned. But remember," he continued, letting his voice harden, "you will be safe only as long as you are within this circle. Do not leave it for any reason!"

Jodi and Martin each nodded, setting their packs on the ground. "We need drinking water," Jodi requested, pointing to the spring beyond the circle's edge. "Can we get it there?"

"I will leave you this," the magician said as he

77

pulled a crystal bottle from his bag and set it on the moss near Jodi. "It will last until I return. I cannot protect the spring because it flows outward, and evil could creep up to you within the water. Have you understood?"

"Yes," both Jodi and Martin said.

"Will you remember all I've told you?"

"Yes sir," they both agreed.

"Ric," Waymond said gravely, "are you ready to attempt your task?"

Eric straightened, holding the Horn of Meet against his chest. "Ready, sir!"

"Good. When we meet again, be prepared for the final battle against the Bane and his slaves."

"I will," Eric declared.

Waymond smiled to each of the three children and began making his way westward. With a wave, Eric turned around. Rapidly he went toward the north, moving as stealthily as a hunter.

Jodi and Martin watched them go with deep regret. They felt abandoned. Jodi resented their situation so much that she sat down on the ground with a plump and began poking at the moss with one finger. "I wish we knew what we're supposed to do here," she said, pouting.

"Yeah," Martin groused. "Some adventure—just sitting in a circle." He plopped down beside his sister and began to draw in the dirt.

To add to their gloom, the gray day was fading into a dreary night. Rain soon began to fall. The brother and sister pulled their blankets out and huddled under them as huge drops of rain pelted down from the lowering, dark clouds.

"Wish I had a warm, dry spot to lay my head," Martin sighed as only a tired, nine-year-old can sigh.

"Here, Martin," Jodi said, patting her lap. "You can put your head here."

He did so as his sister pulled the blankets closer over them. The blankets, however, did not keep out the rain. Soon, both children were soaked and chilled—and thoroughly miserable. The night ahead promised to be dark and mournful indeed.

Chapter 6

Night of Terror

odi and Martin shivered under their wet blankets as black-wet-blackness settled into the Forest. Soon, all light was gone. Not a star pierced the thick rain clouds overhead. Even the waxing moon was completely hidden as the cold, heavy raindrops splashed onto the children's hair and trickled down their unhappy faces. To make matters worse, the chilly breeze was filled with eye-stinging smoke and the smell of rot.

They miserably huddled together for a long while before remembering that Waymond had given each of them a light. Martin thought of his first and pulled the long, silver flashlight from his pack. He turned it on until Jodi drew forth her candlestick and set it before them on the soggy moss.

"Shine," she whispered through chattering teeth, "*please* shine."

A flame flickered from atop the candle, illuminating the ground on which they sat. The light made it seem that they were sitting inside a transparent dome; inside was a yellow glow over green grass and moss, while outside was a world of blackness. They could not even see the branches overhead or the raindrops until they fell into the light. They shivered, wet to the skin from head to toe.

Then it began: doom . . . doom . . . *doom!* Hollow, heavy thuds beat through the Forest, vibrating the earth on which the children huddled: doom . . . doom . . . *doom!*

Stammering from the coldness, Martin asked, "What's th-th-that?"

Jodi's eyes grew round, and she drew the candlestick closer to them. "I don't know," she answered, her voice barely a whisper. They turned to look toward the Forest behind the boulder.

Doom . . . doom . . . doom . . . DOOM! The great thudding blows were few at first, then came more frequently. Moments of silence followed before the sounds were repeated: doom . . . doom . . . doom . . . DOOM! It sounded as though heavy objects were striking something very solid.

Gradually the sounds grew more frequent and began coming from several points in the tongue of Forest that ran down to the magic circle: doom-DOOMdoomdoomDOOM!

Suddenly it dawned on Jodi what was happening. "The Slashes must be chopping down the strip of Forest we came through to get here," she whispered to Martin as chill bumps crowded onto her skin. She imagined the Slashes attacking the ribbon of trees that remained between the two large fields of stumps and burnings. She realized their work inevitably would lead them to the circle!

DoomDOOMDOOMdoom . . . doomDOOM! The blows rained faster now, followed by a prolonged crashing sound as a tree toppled to the earth. Immediately, a hoarse roar thundered through the sodden woods—a vulgar victory grunt from the Slashes to show they had conquered one of the giant trees. Martin and Jodi shivered.

The sounds became louder as more and more Slashes came to work. Within an hour several more crashes burst through the Forest, followed by long groaning cries as tree trunks broke from their hewn stumps. It sounded as though the trees fell in agony, and each fall was answered by the victory grunt of the woodcutters.

Doom . . . doom . . . doom! the chopping blows came from a point nearer the circle in which the children waited, holding onto each other.

"They're coming closer," Martin whispered. He wiped raindrops from his eyes and began to wonder what the Slashes looked like.

"Most likely they're cutting their way along the tongue of the Forest," Jodi said, trying to sound matter-of-fact and brave. But she did not in the least feel brave. She glanced at the rain-washed line drawn in the dirt. She wondered, could a mere line keep out the beasts who were cutting the Forest?

Then a new sound began—a groaning, grunting chant: "Ho-eee-O! Ho-eee-Oo!" Each grunt was followed by a deep sliding sound that made the ground beneath the children tremble. "Ho-eee-O! Ho-eeee-Oo!"

"Th-th-they're d-d-dragging trees," Martin stuttered, clinging to Jodi.

Indeed, they were. And when the Slashes had a mound stacked high, an orange fireball burst upward, shattering the shadows. Its flare was followed by a red glow that crept through the Forest, pursued by the peculiar smoke. A moaning filled the air as the fire brightened in the distance through the trees. The moaning was like wind flowing or water rushing: It was the sound of great beings dying. As the evil flames licked around the stacked trunks, the moan seeped forth louder and louder. The sound made the children tremble. On and on and on went the moaning as the red glow from the burning leaped up to the gray clouds billowing over the tops of the surviving trees.

Closer and louder the sounds of chopping came now. DOOM . . . DOOMDOOM . . . DOOM-DOOMDOOM! Jodi and Martin could hear the mutterings of the woodcutters as they rested between blows of their heavy axes. They could hear the curses as the Slashes pushed and shoved one another to take turns hewing the trunks of the hated trees. They could hear the angry words and vile names the Slashes called one another as they dragged the fallen trees to a burning place they were making quite near the clearing. "HO-EEE-O! HO-EEEE-OO!" came the sliding chant.

Soon, the flare from another orange fireball and the glow of another great fire lit the Forest around the two shivering children. The tree trunks, branches, and leaves all seemed to drip with blood-red light. Flickering light bathed Jodi and Martin and their clearing. It fired the water in their crystal bottle a bright crimson red. And the smoke of the dying trees made their eyes burn and sting as though a Stench were sitting next to them

In fact, Stenches had come—and Reeks too. The Stenches had returned to continue their fouling of the Apple. When they found the spring was clean once more, they shrank away. They were afraid that some overpowering good had returned to the Forest despite their master's might. They lingered in the Forest's shadows, slowly blinking their huge, pale-green eyes. But then the light from the burnings grew bright

83

enough for them to see that the spring was guarded only by two children in a circle. So, when more of their kind arrived, they crept forth to leap into the spring with their muddy, befouled feet.

Jodi stifled a cry as she turned toward the sound of water splashing. She immediately smelled the stink and saw the mud and trash flung down by the Stenches. Martin took his eyes from the red glow and looked around at the Stenches.

"Hey, you!" Martin shouted quite bravely, snatching up his flashlight. "Stop that!" He shined his light toward the Stenches. They froze and cowered in the beam of white light, lifting their scummy shoulders and slimy arms to hide their eyes.

The Stenches soon saw, however, that Martin did not have the power to leave his circle. They laughed a bubbling, gurgling laugh among themselves and defiantly resumed churning the ground around the spring. They laughed louder when they saw Martin stand and come to the edge of his circle, shouting, "Hey! Hey, I said stop that!" The Stenches avoided his beam of light and continued jumping up and down to muddy and roil and ruin the spring. And their smell grew and grew until Martin could stand it no more. He drew back from the edge of the circle and dejectedly sat down.

Reeks came with the smoke to the sound of their fellow beasts at the spring. They laughed shrilly, sort of a "EeeeH-huh-huh-HUH!", when they saw that a party was beginning.

With foul fingers the thin Reeks wove their threads of evil smelling smoke around the clearing and down to the spring. The flowers that had sprung up there wilted and turned brown almost instantly. The Reeks soon had spread smoke all over the ground, withering the grass and moss. Jodi and Martin wet cloths and wrapped them around their noses and mouths to keep out the odor of the Reeks and Stenches. When the creatures saw them do that, they laughed all the louder and pranced up to the circle. There, they hovered, grinning horribly and laughing and pointing with spidery fingers dripping mud.

"AArp!" a gurgling growl came from the Forest. "What's goin' on 'ere?"

The Reeks and Stenches cowered as a huge, humpbacked, hairy beast came from the Forest. In one paw he carried a tremendous ax. The lesser things drew back, pointing at the children in the circle.

The Slash—for the beast was one (a foreman, in fact)—lumbered with thudding steps to the edge of the circle. "What've we got 'ere?" he said with a leer, turning his head left and right so both of his bulging, widely spaced eyes could study the children. Slack lipped, he drooled from around long, yellow-brown fangs. His oily hair reeked of smoke; his eyes burned red in his great head. " 'Eey!" he roared toward the Forest where the DOOM-DOOM-DOOM of ax blows still rang forth. "Come 'ere an' see what's been left!" His voice rumbled so loudly that nearby leaves quivered. Soon, the sound of many other heavy footsteps came through the besieged Forest.

One of the spindly Stenches sidled up to the foreman Slash. "Partyyyy?" it squealed, rubbing its mud-dripping, long hands together. "Partyyyy?"

The Slash turned his head back and forth, scowling at the Stench, whom he did not like. "Gnar!" he growled, shoving away the Stench. "If a party's to be 'ad, it's *us* who'll 'ave it! Gnar!" More and more of the beastly Slashes came down to the clearing, resting their huge double-bladed axes on their beefy, hairy shoulders. "Party's up!" the foreman yelled. "Knock off an' join in!" He waved one paw to the others of his crew who were just coming down.

The blaze of the nearest burning now was leaping as high as the upper branches of the Forest. The clearing was lit bright red. In the glow the children cowered, unable to speak or move. They could only stare at the scene around them.

"But *'e'll* get mad 'f we don't finish this strip of Forest tonight," a particularly large, baleful Slash warned the foreman.

"Nawr, 'e'll let us 'ave some fun," the foreman snarled, turning toward Jodi and Martin. He leaned toward them, drooling, " 'E's never minded when we 'ave fun with such *tidbits* as these 'ere an' like 'em kids back in tha caves!"

"Let's get to it then," another Slash rumbled, glad to lay down his ax. He rubbed his paws together as he went to the circle. "Who'll begin?"

"*I* will!" the foreman growled, roughly shoving the other Slash away.

" 'Ere now, who're yer shovin'?" the second Slash snarled, pushing back.

The foreman snatched up his ax and would have chopped off the other's head had not the largest Slash stepped in. "Who's the enemy 'ere?" he bellowed. They all three turned toward Jodi and Martin.

"Hup, now, me hearties," the foreman called, motioning to the group of Slashes. "Round 'n round we go 'til we break the ring!"

The Slashes lined up around the magic circle. With their heads turned inward to glower at the children, they began to march around the ring. Around and around they went: right hoof, left hoof, right hoof— hop, hop, thud! . . . right, left, right—hop, hop, thud!

Night of Terror

Then, they began to bellow a coarse song, their hooves thudding down at the end of each line:

Song of the Slashes

Break your bones,
make you moans;
when you cries,
tear your eyes!

On your head
we will tread;
bite your face,
make you race!

For we're the Slashes,
boom, boom, boom!
All good we gashes,
boom, boom, boom!

Round and round
we will pound,
'til your blood
be cold mud!

Hack it all,
big and small;
all goes in
to the din!

All hope we dashes,
doom, doom doom!
'cause we're the Slashes,
doom, doom, doom!!

As the circle of beasts cried the last "Doom!" they all leaped toward the children, snarling and drooling. Each hoped to be the first to devour one of the succulent morsels shrinking in fear before them.

But with a deafening roar and blinding flash of white light, a circular tower of lightning shot up from the ring. Cries followed howling cries as the Slashes were burned, singed, scorched, and deafened. They fell back in turmoil, holding their eyes and ears, staggering around and banging into one another. Their power, they found, had not broken—or even dented—the greater power that protected the circle. Jodi and Martin breathed their first full breath in a long time.

"Gnar!" the foreman growled, so angry that he could have hewn one of the trees with his yellowed fangs. "The Song didn't break it! Any o' you boys know another more dire?"

Wagging, shaggy heads answered no.

"Well, garn! We'll have to let the boss deal with 'em," the foreman snarled, "unless. . . ." He turned slowly to the Reeks and Stenches lingering nearby, still hoping for a better end to the party. "Unless one o' you stinkin' things knows a way."

The Stenches and Reeks eagerly slunk forward, dripping ooze and slime and smoke. The head Stench was a particularly foul thing, bred in the darkest swamp ever made by his master. He slithered to the circle and leered at the children. The fact that they were clinging together in obvious love for each other greatly annoyed the Stench. He hung his head and hissed as a slimy mold dripped from his lips.

"Surrre, wee'llll tryyy," the Stench slobbered. He motioned with one scummy hand to the others of his kind and to the Reeks hovering nearby. The foul beings ringed the magic circle four deep. Slowly they began to drift around and around, casting off a stench and reek so disgusting that even the Slashes moved away, holding their snouts shut. This is what the Reeks and Stenches sang:

Song of the Reeks and Stenches

When it's beauty you seek,
into your nose we'll reek;
just try to make it fair,
we'll stink and stench the air!

Loveliness your choosing?
We'll send slime there oozing!
Want dawn to come alighting?
We'll send smoke benighting!

Should flowers come hither,
with our touch we'll wither;
all good things He blesses
we'll ruin with dark messes!

Tired of our wild trashing?
We'll set your teeth to gnashing!
Tired of our befouling?
We'll send you 'way a-howling!

With that the Reeks and Stenches slithered faster, hissing and howling with laughter. Round and round they flew, trailing smoke and stench until they were certain they had ruined the magic of the ring. Jodi and Martin held their breaths as the creatures drew themselves up to plunge shrieking into the circle and consume them.

But when the creatures swooped down upon the circle, the tower of light erupted once more. Sparks flew and leaped among the Stenches and Reeks with a great crackling. Their howls of laughter turned to howls of pain, and the smoke and foul odors flew backward.

"Gnar and double *gnar!*" the Slash foreman growled, shaking his huge ax at the Stenches and Reeks. "You're as useless as I've always said you was! Now we'll have to leave 'em 'ere for the Murks to tease 'til the master comes." Snarling and gnashing his fangs, the Slash called, "Murks! Where be you, you slinkin' shadows? I can feel the fear o' these tidbits, so I know you're 'ere." He and the other Slashes turned this way and that. First one, then more and more pools of shadow crept from the darker depths of the Forest into the red glare flickering over the giant tree trunks. The shadows slunk across the Forest floor and gathered near the charmed circle.

"Ah, there you is, my master's pets," the Slash foreman hissed sarcastically. "Come now an' see 'f you 'ave any more luck than we in breakin' this 'ere cursed ring." With that he hoisted his stained ax, set off up the slope of the hill past the lichen-covered boulder, and clumped into the forest. "Come on, boys; let's leave 'em to it!"

"EE-oo-um! Ee-oo-um! Ee-oo-um!" chanted the woodcutters as they went to resume their work of hewing the trees. Soon, the Reeks and Stenches also went elsewhere, seeking fresh air to foul and clear water to fill with trash and slime. Jodi and Martin opened their eyes as the beastly sounds and smells faded away. They began to breathe again as they looked around. "The circle held," Jodi whispered wonderingly, afraid to raise her voice lest the Murks hear the fear in it.

"But will it keep out the shadows?" Martin asked, hastily letting go of Jodi's arm to pick up his flashlight.

Jodi grasped her candlestick. "Please burn and keep away the Murks," she begged it. Its flame flickered into life as Martin turned on his flashlight.

Thickly toward the circle came the Murks, slinking and slithering from tree trunk to hollow. A great many of them drew up behind the boulder and peered around its edges at the two lights inside the magic ring. Many more came flowing up the plateau from the grassland below where they had been sent to guard against the return of any animals or Zooks, whom they greatly feared.

The Murks soon began to join one huge shadow who seemed to be their leader. It was, in fact, the favorite pet of the Murks' master, who, with great difficulty, had lured it from the depths of the Caves of Rainath in the northland. It could grow large, as large as a cave, and could become as dark as a cave's darkest dark—which is what it now proceeded to do.

It grew and grew as the children watched it through widening eyes. Adding lesser Murks to its powerful shadow, the leader soon towered up and around the magic circle. The children began to doubt that the ring could keep out such a power, for it rose up like the night itself and seemed to have all the fears of darkness within it. It closed out all sounds and shut out all sights, even the red glow of the nearby burnings. Surrounded by the shadow the children quickly forgot where they were and even who they were. They tried to call up memories of sunny days, of their home and friends, of pleasant things to eat and do—but all their efforts were in vain. They even forgot Waymond and their mission.

"Maybe we should run," Martin whispered, almost wild with fright.

"Run where?" Jodi asked helplessly, trembling as she clung to Martin.

He began to cry, for never had Jodi not been able to comfort his fears. But now, he saw, she was just as frightened as he was—and that fact made him even more afraid.

"Oh, why did we come here?" he cried. "I wish . . . I wish . . . oh, I don't even know what to wish!"

Jodi stared into the candle flame, watching its white and blue glow. It seemed to grow in her imagination, and soon she could see nothing but its brightness. She began to smile. "I know what to wish," she softly told Martin as her trembling stopped. "I wish the dawn would come."

Hearing the sudden absence of fear in her voice, the great cave shadow redoubled its efforts to drive them out of the circle. Chills of gloom it gathered from far around and flung against the ring. Waves of dark it sought and hurled toward the children. Murks came to its call by the hundreds and swirled around and around.

"Don't look at them, Martin," Jodi said, regaining both her memory and her courage. "Just watch the candle's light and wait for the dawn."

The cave darkness could not stand being ignored; it moaned and sighed, gathering all the whispers of nighttime, all the strange and unnerving groanings and gratings of darkness. It sent the sounds against the circle time and time again, hovering above it all with its empty black might. But its efforts were useless because the children sat close together and continued to stare into the small bright flame. Martin gradually sank onto Jodi's lap and went peacefully to sleep.

The long hours of the night crept by. The Murks grew weary, for their strength was great only when fed by the fear of their prey. They settled into a hovering wreath about the circle, hoping the courage of the children would fail. It did not, however, and at last a grayness edged into the eastern sky. The rain

93

stopped. The clouds seemed to grow thinner, and the light from the east became stronger.

"Look," Jodi said, rousing Martin. "The clouds and smoke are parting, and there's the sun!"

Martin awoke with an effort, the thought of the bright flame still strong in his mind. When he looked where his sister pointed, he saw the red face of the sun peering over the dark green roof of the remaining Forest. The sunlight sent the Murks slinking away.

"We've done it!" Jodi proudly cried as she stood up stiffly. She dragged Martin up beside her and hugged him as they watched the sun rise higher to become yellow and bright. "We've survived the night! We've met the test!" Happy, and crying tears of joy, they danced around and around in the magic circle and watched the sun rise. "We've done it!" Jodi again cried proudly.

Chapter 7

Grandfather Obit

Congratulations!" a kindly voice greeted them from nearby.

The children blinked in surprise and noticed an old man of gentle appearance. He was sitting cross-legged on the lichen-covered boulder. How long he had been there, they had no idea. It seemed he had come suddenly, yet he was so settled that he could have been sitting there for quite some time.

"Congratulations on your victory," the old man said nicely, smiling at them. "You mastered your fears *very* well and have admirably overcome all danger. You have a right to be proud of yourselves!"

Jodi eyed him suspiciously, but frazzled Martin felt comforted by his soothing voice. Jodi asked, "Who are you? Are you the King?"

The old man laughed easily and picked a bit of lint from his gray, red-edged robe. "In a way, I suppose I am," he purred, sitting up regally. They thought his face was kindly, though his eyes were difficult to see since they kept moving. He stroked his long, soft white hair and neatly trimmed beard. "I am Grandfather Obit, and you may call me Obbie if you wish." He smiled warmly.

"What are you doing here?" Jodi inquired, trying to maintain her suspicious frame of mind. She remembered Waymond's warnings—though they did not seem to apply to this friendly looking old man.

"I came to investigate the terrible sounds I heard last night. I was afraid the fierce creatures who now roam the Forest had harmed someone, so I came to see if I could be of assistance."

"You sure can!" Martin cried without thinking. He started to run to the old man, who held out his arms to receive him with a smile.

Jodi grabbed her brother by one arm and held him back. "Just a minute," she snapped at him. "Don't you remember? Waymond told us . . ."

"Oh, but I'm sure your guide didn't mean that you were not to come to *me,*" the old man said gently, smiling to Martin.

"Well, you're not going anywhere," Jodi instructed Martin, shaking his arm. She glared at Grandfather Obit.

He winced. "You wound me, young lady. How can you not trust an old man such as I? Do I not look kindly? And," he added, reaching toward a bag behind him on the boulder, "I even brought you good food, for I thought you might be hungry after a night in a horrid forest such as this." He turned and slowly opened the bag as Martin strained forward to see what might be in it. Jodi felt her mouth begin to water at the mere mention of food, for she and Martin had eaten nothing since lunch the day before.

Then she tensed. "No; we mustn't." She folded her arms.

The old man turned back to face them and gazed sadly at her. "Now, *think* for just a moment, if you will. You don't know what I have here in my bag, but I assure you that it's something very good for you to eat. Would your guide not want you to share a fine breakfast with a lonely old man? Would he be so cruel as to deny me the company of two brave children during my morning meal? Would he be so heartless as to deny you good, nutritious food? Please consider all sides of the question before you answer."

Jodi frowned uncertainly at Martin, who scowled hungrily back at her. She could tell that he already agreed with Grandfather Obit. Jodi wondered: Did Waymond's instructions cover this possibility? Or had he meant they should remain in the circle only if danger came? Though he had said they should not leave the circle until he returned, he had not left them any food and they had none with them. But then again, neither she nor Martin had asked for food; when they asked for water, Waymond had given them enough for their needs. But . . . well. . . . Her frown deepened. "No," she said at last, but less firmly than before.

Again, the old man appeared wounded. His face took on a sad expression as he gazed at her with apparent concern for her well-being. "Please . . . think again. You're not being logical! Isn't it logical to accept help when it is offered?" He turned at the waist and drew from the bag hard-boiled eggs and a jar of orange juice. He set the eggs and jar carefully on the boulder. Next, he withdrew from the bag a container of biscuits stained yellow with butter and a rasher of bacon also in a container. That the containers were like those littering the spring went unnoticed by the children. He set the open containers on the boulder so that they could see the food.

"As you undoubtedly can see," Grandfather Obit said gently, "it is good food. Now, would your guide make you *starve* yourselves—just because of some silly old *rule?*" He looked gravely at them, then spoke in a commanding tone much like their mother might use when she wanted to make them do something. "Think about it! Aren't there exceptions to *all* rules? And weren't rules made to be broken by someone brave enough to do so? Just think, if someone hadn't been brave, no one ever would have eaten an oyster or an artichoke. And haven't you heard that at one time, ignorant and old-fashioned fools said, 'If man was supposed to fly, he'd have been born with wings'? But people did fly, and nothing bad happened to them! See? All rules fall by the wayside when something better comes along. So please now, won't you come have breakfast with me? *Why* do you continue to deny yourselves food that you want?" He recrossed his legs as he gazed at them in a perplexed, concerned sort of way. When they still hesitated, he slowly began eating.

The food certainly looked good. The orange juice was bright orange, as though it had just been squeezed from delicious oranges. The biscuits were tall and just barely browned on top. Creamy butter oozed from the middles of the biscuits. Jodi's and Martin's mouths watered more and more.

Not only did the food look good; it smelled delightful! The scent of the bacon came to them, tickling their noses. The biscuits smelled of warm ovens where breads bake until they are just right for butter to melt all down into them. Even the fresh, tangy odor of the orange juice wafted to them.

"Come on!" Martin urged, tugging on Jodi's hand. "It can't hurt to step just outside the circle and have some food. We can jump back if anything goes wrong."

"Listen to your brother!" the old man said eagerly, holding out a biscuit. "I assure you, you won't have to come far from the circle. You won't really be much outside it—only a little bit, and what can one little step harm? Think how much that little step will gain you!" He smiled a disarming smile, holding out the biscuit.

"Well . . .," Jodi hesitated, alternately frowning and losing her frown. "Maybe it wouldn't hurt just to sample the food." She went to the edge of the circle. Looking toward the food, she held out one hand.

"Go on," Martin urged, feeling really hungry.

"Come on," Grandfather Obit said gently, holding the biscuit close to himself so she would have to step out of the circle to take it.

"I don't know," Jodi said weakly, her expression clouded with doubt. She knew in her heart that this stranger was not to be trusted, but hunger overrode what her heart told her. She murmured, "But Waym . . ."

"Oh, bother what your guide said," the old man snapped, biting into the biscuit. "I've fed many children, some of them Zooks. And every one of them wanted to eat with me."

Jodi remained partially unconvinced, remembering Waymond's sternness.

"Jodi Kay Westphall," the old man suddenly said, "I'm surprised at you!" Before she could ask how he knew her name, he continued. "You are the very one who so often has said that '*they*' have no right to tell you what to do. You've felt unneeded and unloved by your parents. You have felt they didn't understand you or want you around sometimes—isn't that right?" She nodded numbly. "You've even said that you *hated* them, that you'd run away—if you were *brave* enough." He sat back, smiling as she stood stunned before him. In a more kindly voice he said, "Well, I'm offering you not only food and companionship but myself, for I *need* you. I need your good wishes. It hurts me to think that you can't trust me, that you

would be so unkind as to deny a lonely old man the
pleasure of your charming company—just because
some silly old rule says you *mustn't*." He sneered the
word "mustn't" as though it were something nasty.
"Do what *you* choose to do," he went on. "You're old
enough to decide for yourself what's best for you—
aren't you?" He lifted one gray eyebrow in question,
challenging her. "Come on and *show* them!"

That did it. "Yes, I am old enough to decide!" Jodi
said firmly. With a giant step, she left the circle. Martin quickly followed.

Nothing happened immediately to make them regret their choice. The food tasted as good as the children had imagined it would. Close to it, it smelled
even better than it had from within the circle. They
wondered why they had waited so long to accept the
old man's kindness. They ate and ate, biscuits and
bacon, eggs and juice . . . but strangely they became
neither full nor satisfied. In fact, their hunger in-
creased.

"Have some more juice," Grandfather Obit urged,
holding out the bottle. Jodi momentarily recalled that
she had seen a pile of such bottles in the trash befouling the spring below. However, she dismissed the fact
as a coincidence and held out her glass for more of the
tangy drink. As she drank, she frowned because her
thirst grew.

"And you, Martin, have some more bacon. I know
how fond you are of bacon!" the old man said, taking
out another package of the crisply fried meat. When
he had given the strips to Martin, he wadded up the
package and tossed it onto the ground. Martin looked
at the litter, but he said nothing for fear of offending
their benefactor.

They ate and ate, but still they could not be satisfied. Though the smell and taste were good, fill their

stomachs the food would not. Finally, all they wanted to do was to catch up on the sleep they had lost during the terrible night.

"Sleepy, my children?" Grandfather Obit asked in his kindly way. "Well, when you're all done here, I'll take you on a short walk."

Jodi started to say something about the food not being satisfying, but she kept silent, thinking it was *her* fault. She did manage to protest weakly, "But we have to wait here for . . . for our guide."

"Oh, you can wait for him at my home," the old man said easily. *"If* he comes back—and I doubt that he will—he won't mind coming a bit farther to where you are."

"You don't think he'll come back for us like he said he would?" Martin asked. In his mind he found himself beginning to dislike Waymond.

"Of course not," Grandfather Obit answered with a chuckle. "So come along now." He climbed off the boulder and quickly stuffed the bag under his robe. He walked a few steps away, ignoring the food containers lying about on the ground.

Jodi hesitated . . . but her disappointment and resentment at being left out of the action without a heroic part to play filled her with anger at Waymond. And, after all, he had not offered to leave them any food! "Just a moment," she said, going to get her pack from the circle.

"Oh, you won't . . .," the old man began. But Jodi already had discovered what he was about to say. She could not reenter the circle.

Martin burped openly and sneered at his sister, then sauntered to do what she had not been able to do. But an invisible wall, the same that had kept out the Slashes and Reeks and Stenches, repelled him. He fell back and landed hard on his seat.

The old man instantly threw back his head and laughed hideously, wagging his beard defiantly toward the sky. He abruptly turned upon the children with a jeering glare, and they saw that his kindly expression was gone. "Come along," he said in a voice of ownership, *"now!"*

Jodi and Martin immediately realized their mistake. "No!" Jodi screamed. She seized Martin's hand and ran with him in tow around the circle to flee downhill.

A screech burst through the air from the trees above. It was the cry of Jodi's eagle, which had spent the night frozen in terror among the branches. Now, it frantically was flying away from something it feared more than Slashes, Stenches, and even fire itself.

Jodi and Martin turned and were horrified to see a Wrath appear. *"Aaiieesskreecht!"* the bird's blood-chilling cry tore the Forest stillness. The huge creature flapped heavily in pursuit of the eagle. But the smaller bird dove under tree branches and sped westward. Before Jodi could drag her trembling brother into cover behind nearby trees, the Wrath wheeled back. For a moment, it blocked out the sun with its enormous wings. Then down it dove, extending its scythe-like talons.

"Runnn!" Jodi cried, tugging on Martin. Her brother, though, was riveted to the ground with fright. The Wrath plummeted upon them, appearing to grow larger each second. It snatched up Jodi in one sharp-clawed foot and Martin in the other. As its talons snapped shut in the garments on their backs, they heard and felt the huge bird flapping hard. The Wrath's broad wings whipped them with gusts of wind as it lifted them up, then hovered above its master. As the children stared down from forty feet above the clearing, they saw how much the old man had changed.

Hatred and unspeakable scorn lashed from his eyes as he shook a gnarled fist up at them. "Take them," he screeched to the Wrath, "to Crossingsend and dump them in!"

"Waymond will get you for this!" Jodi cried down, her bravery returning despite the height from which the Wrath dangled them.

Grandfather Obit cackled, shaking his beard in defiance at the sky. He glared up at her. "Don't you recognize my bag?" he sneered in an awful way, holding up the object he had been carrying beneath his robe. Only then did the children recognize the carpetbag of their friend, Waymond.

"And how do you suppose I got it?" Obit snarled. "You don't imagine he *gave* it to me, do you? Besides, he'd never help you two now; you've *betrayed* him!"

"There are still the Zooks," Martin yelled down. "They'll come rescue us when our friend calls them, no matter what you do!"

With a jerk, Obit reached into the magician's bag. As spite lit his face, he pulled forth the Horn of Meet and shook it at Martin. "Recognize this toy?" the old man jeered. "You'll soon join its former owner in my dungeons with the other children who are learning to obey me!" He laughed, throwing back his head, then glowered up at Jodi and Martin. "And do not imagine that the foolish Zooks could have harmed *me* anyway. I've turned many of them—and lots of weak, rebellious, and needful children, like you—into my Sneaks. Soon, like all my slaves, *you* will help do my work of remaking this miserable kingdom into a place of desolation where my beasts and pets can live as they please. Then, never more will we be bothered by any of your, or the former king's, stupid ideas!" He cackled loudly, waving to the Wrath to carry the children away.

"*Aaiieeesskreeechttt!*" the Wrath shrieked, echoing the old man's laughter. It flapped hard, climbed above the trees, and flew quickly northward over the slashed and burned land. The children's hearts sank.

Helplessly, they looked down at the spreading blanket of smoke. It covered the entire center of the Forest, and they barely could see the edges of green lying far away. It appeared that the work of the Slashes soon would be done, and all the Forest would be chopped down.

As Jodi and Martin flew, dangling from the Wrath's talons, they looked down on a few places where a breeze had torn the veil of smoke. In those places stumps appeared, tiny dots on a trampled land. Flames from scattered burnings often shot up through the smoky pall, and the stench of destruction burned in their nostrils. As the children thought that now they would be forced to speed the calamity, they began to cry.

The wide wings of the Wrath beat up and down on either side of them for a long while. Breathing was difficult in the cold air, and constantly their fear was fanned as they thought what would happen if the Wrath should drop them. Oh, how they regretted stepping outside the circle, even for food! Their regrets, however, did not affect the Wrath, for it kept up a steady flight for miles above the smoke.

They soon came above a yawning network of black-shadowed canyons. The smoke lingered at the edges of the gorges and seemed to be holding back from where the earth dropped inward upon itself. A few tall, rugged old cypress trees poked upward beside the canyon edges; apparently they were remnants of better days. The bottoms of the narrow gashes in the earth were so deep that sunlight was not in them. But even blacker than the canyon shadows were the mouths of caves that pierced the lower walls alongside the five rivers flowing within the network. There seemed to be a great many of the black-mouthed caves, and from several of them black smoke trickled. The Wrath circled lower and lower, and it became obvious that they had reached the creature's destination.

Jodi watched the canyons and caves drawing nearer, and she began to struggle. Desperately she reached up and snatched a handful of hard-edged feathers from the breast of the Wrath.

"Aasskreecht!" it cried in surprise and pain. Instinctively, it unclenched its talons. Jodi and Martin dangled for a moment on the tips of two of the sharp hooks. Then their clothing slipped off. They plunged downward from many hundreds of feet in the air. Down . . . down . . . down they fell, screaming, spinning slowly head over heels. Down . . . down . . . down . . . and down. The fall seemed to go on forever.

Chapter 8

Reginald Potterpost Baskenberry

It seemed to Jodi and Martin that they fell from the sky for a very long time. During that awful fall the wind whistled past their bodies, the blur of the earth rushed up, and many memories flashed through their minds. Regrets and painful experiences were among the memories, but the children were surprised at how many good things they recalled. They discovered that far more good, happy events had happened to them than sad, miserable ones. It then seemed a great pity to be about to die, and they bitterly regretted having listened to Obit.

On impulse, Jodi suddenly screamed as loudly as she could, "*Please,* King we've never seen, save us!" As tears were torn from her eyes by the wind, she felt a strange confidence spread within her.

Martin heard her shout and woke from a trance of fear. Her words gave him hope. So, as they tumbled, he struggled to reach out and clasp hands with her— with difficulty, naturally, for they were falling quite fast.

Then several things happened all at once: Brown

cliff tops whisked past; the children closed their eyes; and the tip of a grandfatherly cypress tree rose between them. Soft, green branches tore against their clasped arms, slowing them as they fell among the boughs. They came to a stop on a swaying, jerking branch with their hands still locked together.

"Are we dead?" Jodi whispered, not daring to open her eyes. "Or did the King save us?"

"I think he must have," Martin returned, afraid to move. Slowly, he opened his eyes. "Look, we've landed in a tree!"

Jodi's eyes fluttered open. "Ohhh!" she moaned, shutting her eyes when she saw how much farther it was to the rocky canyon floor. Below the children sloped the thick needle-leaves of the cypress, which grew straight up from the canyon bottom. There, a river rushed beside the fluted base of the tree.

Jodi gripped Martin's hands more tightly as they continued to sway gently back and forth, draped over the limber limb. Slowly, the limb began to droop downward until their feet dangled to within inches of another bough. "Ohhh!" Jodi moaned as she felt their hands slipping down the limb. "I'm *dizzy!*"

"If you're so scared *now*," Martin asked impatiently, looking for the best way down, "where'd you get the courage to pull that Wrath's feathers and call to the King?"

"I grabbed the Wrath because I thought it'd be better to end it quickly, rather than be slaves forever!" she groaned. "And I shouted because Waymond said the King was very powerful." She swallowed hard, trembling with her eyes closed.

"Silly," Martin said, "you've just fallen *hundreds* of feet, and you're afraid of a few feet more? Come on," he added quickly. "I'm good at climbing trees. I'll lead you down."

He made her hold onto the tree limb over which

they were draped while he let go and dropped onto the branch below their feet. Then he guided her body as she lowered herself with several more "Ohhhs" to the thickly leaf-needled branch beside him. "Don't knock me off!" he commanded. "And *do* open your eyes!"

Hearing voices below them—quarrelsome voices—she opened her eyes and hissed, "Shhh." They clung to the rough, gray trunk and listened.

"Snitch-itch, they must've fallen in a ditch!" a high, angry voice jabbered rapidly.

"Twitch-switch, bet they're splattered like pitch!" another squeaked, laughing in a snivelling way.

"Better grab'em, nab'em," a deeper voice growled, "or the master'll jab you, stab you, you brainless nameless!"

"You shush, you big Snitch," a higher voice squeaked angrily. "You can't tell us Sneaks what to do! We're trackers, not slackers."

"Yeah, well I was sent to watch you, *gotchu!*" the gruff voice returned. The sound of a blow being struck thunked from below.

Jodi and Martin flattened themselves against the tree trunk like hunted squirrels.

"The Wrath dropped 'em, popped 'em, so let 'im find 'em, bind 'em," a Sneak voice whined.

"Smack!" went the sound of the Snitch's fist as it hit the Sneak. "That'll hold ya, fold ya!" the deeper voice snarled. Sounds of heavy footsteps thudded away up the riverbank.

"Ninny-nanny, you're a granny!" the Sneak's voice whined after the footsteps, which instantly stopped and returned running. Tiny snapping footsteps rattled off down the riverbank with great speed, followed by the thudding footfalls as the Snitch ran in hot pursuit.

"Nice folks we've fallen among," Martin observed

sarcastically. He leaned away from the tree trunk to catch a glimpse of who might be below. What he saw were several small, dark, and ragged forms running helter-skelter away from a tall, shaggy creature with very long arms.

"Can you get me down now?" Jodi pleaded, her eyes closed again.

"Oh, yes," Martin remembered. Taking one of her hands, he led her downward from branch to branch. The many arms of the old cypress were arranged around the trunk much like steps. They were slippery, however, so it took the children a long while to reach the ground. There, Martin peered up and down the canyon. It seemed deserted, so he led Jodi scrambling over the loose rocks toward the water. They knelt to drink.

"Paughh!" Martin spat, slinging water. "*He's* fouled this too."

"Stenches, you mean."

"Stenches, Snitches, who cares?" Martin complained. "I'm thirsty!"

"Not so loud," Jodi hissed. "Do you want them to come back?"

"They may anyhow," Martin guessed, looking around. He saw that the narrow canyon led east to an intersection of at least five canyons. All the cliffs near the intersection were pitted with the dark openings of caves, some big and some not so big. Many of the cave mouths had thick, black smoke dribbling out of them, and Martin assumed the caves to be the homes of the Snitches and Sneaks—and what else he dared not imagine. Taking Jodi's hand, Martin led her at a run up the river, away from the junction toward which the Sneaks had run. When he saw a cave that appeared unused, he headed for it.

Martin climbed up the cliff to the black cave mouth.

While Jodi kept watch below, he peered cautiously into the cave.

"They're coming back!" she warned, scrambling up to join him. Without being able to tell what might be lurking inside, they darted into the cave and hid behind some boulders near the opening.

"Snitches, twitches, bust yer britches!" a voice squeaked from outside. Jodi and Martin's hearts almost stopped, for they thought they had been seen. But it was only a gang of Sneaks and Snitches trooping up the riverbank.

"Here, there, look everywhere!" a gruff voice commanded. "This ain't no game, you creeps with no name!"

Jodi and Martin heard footsteps in large number pass slowly in front of the cave entrance. Several heads with tousled, greasy hair and dirty, sullen faces appeared in the opening. The ones who weren't scratching at their heads were picking their noses. The Sneaks glanced left and right but soon withdrew, afraid to discover what might live in the dark depths. They knew that though their master now ruled the Forest, he still had not had his slaves root out all the wild things that lived in the caves of Crossingsend. So, the Sneaks went on, hurried by several large Snitches with whips.

It was a long while before Jodi and Martin dared stick their heads above the boulders and look around. When they did, it was only because they smelled a strange, earthy smell and heard an ominous voice behind them. "GgrrrooOOwwaugh," the voice purr-roared.

Hair on end, Martin and Jodi hesitated between running into the clutches of the Snitches and seeing what was coming from the dark end of the cave. Two orange, black-slitted eyes appeared, shining in the light from the entrance. "GrroWow," the creature growled, coming closer.

The children were all set to flee when they saw a long, tall cougar walk out, stretching. He stretched all down his back, pressing low in front and high behind; then he stretched low behind and high in front. He blinked sleepily and noticed them. "Hullo," the cat said, switching his long tail. "What's all the ruckus? Fellow can't get a bit of sleep." He sat down and began licking his yellow-brown fur into place with his broad tongue.

"You're a cougar, aren't you?" Jodi stammered. She was not at all sure she wanted to remain in the cave, though the cat did seem familiar.

"Of course," the cat grumped, blinking at her. Then he noticed their obvious fright and did his best to smile. "Don't worry; I'm charmed by the King's spell."

"*The* King?" Martin asked.

"Is there more than one?" the cougar growled, bristling.

Jodi and Martin exchanged uneasy looks, then stared at the cat. Jodi replied, "Well, there are others, but I don't suppose they have the power of *the* King. For example, we believe he saved us from a terrible fall just a while ago."

"Really?" the cat asked, purr-rr-rring. "Tell me about it."

"Okay," Jodi began, "but don't make fun of us for thinking it was the King that saved us."

"Some would call such things luck or coincidence, but *I* know better," the cat assured her.

Jodi went on to describe everything about their journey with Waymond, what they had seen happening to the Forest, and about their fall.

When she finished telling the sad news, the cougar

shook his head slowly. "Ummm, I knew I shouldn't have gone to sleep! But, that's what I get for thinking the magicians could handle everything!" He sighed and stood. "Oh well, if that's the way things are, I might as well get to work!" He set off toward the mouth of the cave.

"Wait!" Jodi said quickly, impulsively grabbing his tail to stop him. With a low growl, he turned. She let go, embarrassed, and went on, "Didn't you hear me say there are Snitches and Slashes, Stenches and Reeks and all the rest?"

"So?" the cat asked, bending back to lick his tail where she had ruffled his fur. "What are such beasts to a warrior such as I? It simply means there's less time to dally."

"But you just can't go rushing off."

"Why not?" he asked, blinking his wide, shining eyes. "They can't hurt *me!*"

"They can too," Martin corrected. "They can throw you in some dark dungeon like they've done to the good children and our friend and like they were going to do to us."

"They? *They,* you say?" the cougar growled with rising temper. "*They* will do nothing of the sort to me!" He flexed long, sharp claws and let his upper lip ripple back to reveal very long, gleaming white fangs.

"Perhaps not," Jodi agreed thoughtfully. "But I've a better idea. Would you guide us to the sorcerer's dungeons? Maybe we can find our friend who was supposed to blow the Horn of Meet and call the Zooks. Or possibly we can find the King. By the way, what does he look like?"

The cat ignored her question, letting his eyes close lazily as he thought. "Yes," he conceded at last. "I could guide you . . . but open battle would be much more to my liking. However, let's hear your plan." He sat back, ready to listen.

"Oh dear," Jodi sighed. "I don't actually have a plan. I just know that our friend and the children need to be found and that Martin and I need a chance to redeem ourselves."

"Redeem yourselves?" the cougar asked. He ambled to the cave's mouth to sit in the sunlight. "Redeem yourselves from what?"

"I told you," Jodi answered impatiently, wishing the cat had a longer memory. "We let ourselves be talked out of Waymond's magic circle by that old man—Grandfather Obit."

"Hm, well, if you broke the magician's instructions I should hope you'd get another chance. Hate to see anyone cast off without a second chance, you know." He began licking one paw, then paused. "Did you say the chief perpetrator of all this trouble is *Obit?*" the cougar spat, slinging his head as though he had a bit of rotten food stuck to a whisker.

"You know him?"

"Oh, yes. A positive snake charmer, that one. Or maybe snake and charmer all in one." He snorted at his own joke and resumed washing one paw as he basked in the sunlight.

"I wouldn't sit there if I were you," Martin warned.

The cat stared at him. "Oh, you wouldn't? Well, watch this!" He strode to the cliff, sprang in an arc to the riverbed, and knelt in a leisurely manner to drink. Even from their hiding place the children could hear him cough. "A-paughh!" he choked, squinching up his eyes. Martin could not keep from snickering. The cougar, though, was not embarrassed; he turned and strolled back to the cliff as though nothing whatsoever were amiss.

115

Gracefully he leaped back into the cave. "Doesn't matter," he said disdainfully as he strolled past them. "Doesn't matter, for now, in the least. I have my own water, which even the Stenches wouldn't *dare* dabble their nasty claws in." He went toward the rear of the cave.

"Water?" Martin inquired, following the cat despite Jodi's efforts to hold him back. After the encounter with Grandfather Obit, she was determined to be very cautious. Martin, however, was extremely thirsty. He went with the cougar to a small, sweet-smelling spring in the back of the cave. He and the animal knelt side by side and drank from the water that bubbled into a bowl-shaped hollow of clean rocks.

The cat licked droplets from his chin and whiskers, blinking his eyes as they adjusted to the darkness. "There now, that's better, isn't it?"

"Very satisfying," Martin replied.

Hearing nothing that sounded as if her brother was being devoured, Jodi felt her way through the darkness and joined him and the cat at the spring. She drank her fill, then groped her way to a seat. "Nice cave you have . . . Say, what is your name?"

"Rude!" the cat chided. "You've come bursting in on me uninvited, so I've a right to know your names first."

Jodi blushed and was glad the cave was so dark that Martin couldn't see her pink cheeks. "My name is Jodi Kay Westphall, and . . ."

"And I'm Martin," Martin added brightly.

"Very pleased to meet you, though the circumstances are not the best, I must say. I am named Reginald Potterpost Baskenberry, but you may call me Reg."

Jodi and Martin laughed. "Haven't we met before?" Jodi asked, hooking her arms around her upraised knees.

"Don't think so," the cougar mumbled, stifling a burp; he had drunk the water too quickly.

"Didn't you appear at our house one day with Waymond?" she persisted.

"Oh, yes. Waymond. How is he anyhow?" the cat purred inquisitively.

"I've *told* you!" Jodi snapped.

"Oh, yes, well, harumph!" the cougar muttered, hiding a belch.

Martin sat crosslegged on the dry floor of the cave. "How'd you get such a long name?"

"Ah, well, you see—or maybe you can't see," Reg laughed, "I am, or was as the case may be, a friend of the King's cooks. One in particular didn't mind my coming around for scraps—not begging, you understand, but simply asking. I shall be very sorry—and very *angry*—if old Obit's done anything to *him*. Proper Englishman that cook is, or was, and he thought I should have a proper English name. So he named me Reginald Potterpost Baskenberry."

The mention of a cook made Martin consider the emptiness of his stomach in spite of eating Obit's food just a few hours earlier. "You, um, wouldn't happen to have . . . ," he began but stopped for fear of being rude.

"Have any food?" Reg ended for him. "I should have plenty in my larder, but I don't quite remember. I've been asleep for several days—had *quite* a feast last week. That's when all the trouble began, when the boundary wardens were full and happy after the springtime festival." He tisked his broad tongue over his long teeth as though chiding himself. "I should have known not to go to sleep after Waymond sent me back. Those magicians! Even they get overconfident and have their blind spots, you know."

"You mentioned a springtime festival," Jodi said. "It was autumn when we came into the Forest."

"Drat and dash that old Obit," Reg snarled. "That'll be more of *his* doing."

"Well, the Stenches and Reeks didn't help matters," Martin glumly added, remembering the way they had withered the flowers and grass.

"I should think not. But they're harmless enough if you know how to handle them."

"And how is that?" Martin asked, hoping to learn some startling battle tactic to use the next time he had to face Obit's slaves.

"Clean 'em up and run 'em out using the King's power, of course!" Reg snarled, and even in the dark they could see the glint of his fangs.

"Oh," Martin said, again wishing he could hurry up and meet the King and maybe get a real sword.

"However," Reg continued in a softer tone, "first things first. I believe it was food you wanted, wasn't it?"

"Yes . . . sir," the children responded.

"Hummmm," the cat purred, walking easily around in the darkness. He rummaged here, rattled stoneware there, and soon returned to lay several things in the children's laps. Jodi was afraid even to touch whatever it was in her lap, but Martin sniffed the aroma and started eating immediately.

"What is it?" Jodi asked warily, holding her hands away from her lap.

Through his stuffed mouth, Martin mumbled, " 'S shi-ken."

"Pigeon, actually," Reg corrected. "From the King's kitchen, no less."

Jodi hesitantly picked up a piece, sniffed it, and began eating. "It's good," she admitted, remembering their last meal with regret.

When they had finished, they washed in the spring and drank its cool, pure water. Seated on rocks near the almost invisible form of Reg, they sighed with contentment. Soon, despite—or because of—their recent fright, they fell fast asleep. Reg, thoughtful cat that he was, laid them gently on the cave floor with fragrant, balsam bough pillows under their heads. There, the brother and sister spent the remainder of the day, asleep but restless.

Bad dreams troubled their slumber; evil scenes recurred, always with Obit in the center of the turmoil. They saw themselves over and over becoming worthless slaves cast to their doom by the pitiless old man. And worst of all, he kept laughing at them.

Chapter 9

Into the Sorcerer's Cave

*M*artin and Jodi awoke exhausted. But the sweet balsam fragrance of their pillows revived them, and they wondered how the branches had gotten under their heads.

"Now," the cougar said from the darkness near them, "to matters next at hand. Are you ready to go?"

"To go where?" Jodi asked shakily, still picturing her vivid dreams and reliving her frightful fall from the sky.

"Here, now, what're you playing at?" the warrior cat asked sharply. "Are you ready to do what you said you wanted to do? Or has Obit infected your minds with fear? He does that well, you know."

Jodi now wished the cougar had a shorter memory, for she did not in the least look forward to exploring the canyons and caves.

"Are you already breaking your resolve to seek redemption?" Reg asked impatiently.

The children immediately stood. Martin took hold of the cat's tail, which he had presented to the boy, and Jodi held onto Martin's shirt as Reg led them out of the darkness of the cave. When they reached the cave's mouth they saw that a dark, dark night had fallen within Crossingsend.

As they followed Reg at a rapid pace alongside the river, down the night-blackened canyon, Jodi felt certain that terrible events were rapidly approaching. It seemed that Obit's voice was somewhere in her mind, trying to break her small courage and enslave her. To cast off her feeling, she experimented with a small prayer: "Powerful King, King who loves children, will you please come with us."

Martin, meanwhile, to break the fearful silence that was feeding his anxiety, whispered aloud, "Reg, why is this place called what it is?"

"All rivers of the Land cross here," Reg quietly explained, "so this is where all crossings end."

"That doesn't make sense," Martin complained, stumbling over a rock.

"Of course it does," Reg snapped, "and watch where your feet go!"

The river gradually broadened, and soon they could hear it joining the rushing currents of several other rivers. The jagged canyon rims, towering far above the stealthy trio, drew back from one another and merged to form the edge of a roughly star-shaped valley. As the threesome walked on in silence, they noticed dim light flickering from the caves that were scattered all around the cliffsides of the valley. Also, they began to hear sounds of squabbling and bickering.

"Careful now," Reg whispered, "step as quietly as I do."

Martin frowned, wondering how he could possibly be as quiet as the cat; except to speak, Reg had not made one sound since they had set out. But Martin followed carefully nevertheless, and the thought of the nearby Snitches and Sneaks made him walk more quietly than he would have imagined possible. He surprised even Jodi.

Having spent two full days and nights tramping through the Forest and sleeping on the ground, the children were very dirty. Their grime now camouflaged them as they flitted from shadow to rock, from boulder to tree and back to shadow. Nary another stone did they disturb as they carefully placed their feet. They both looked and acted like wild things on the prowl.

The caves loomed above them, and the flickering of firelight was now clearly visible from within the rough mouths. Snarling sounds and thrashing noises burst forth frequently. Curses and whines, blows and squeals rent the night, rising louder at times than the splash and gurgle of the mingling rivers. Martin thought it obvious that the Sneaks did not at all get along with the Snitches and, most probably, not even with one another.

As they crept along, Martin at first maintained his courage by remembering that they were on a mission. That thought led to another which really boosted his courage: If Jodi's shout to the King had caused them to be saved from the terrible fall, surely, *surely* the King could send them courage now. Martin found himself repeating, almost with each step, "King, *please* help us do this mission right and not be afraid!" After repeating that request for awhile, Martin began to feel quite brave indeed. He also began to feel that he was doing royal service. And serving the King seemed to mean serving others, like the children being held captive somewhere in Obit's dungeons. He stopped and smiled to himself. "I rather feel like we're the King's men," he whispered toward Jodi, "on our way to do royal battle." She apparently was still too frightened to consider such an idea, for she pointed ahead and hissed at him to keep silent.

They were at the brink of a broad river that blocked their forward progress. They paused for several seconds, and at first the children thought the halt was to enable Reg to look for guards. Then they noticed that the black tip of his yellow-brown tail was twitching in a peculiar way; He was, they saw, reluctant to enter the water.

"Go on, if we must!" Martin urged, feeling as though a thousand evil eyes were upon them. "Let's not stand . . ." Before he could finish, the cat had taken a deep breath and plunged into the water. The children followed, shivering and holding their breath because of the water's coldness. Waist deep, the river's current was swift and powerful. However, they crossed without harm and hid behind a cluster of boulders until most of the water had drained from their clothing.

"I really did *not* need a bath," Reg muttered as they went on.

Martin again started to tell Jodi about his idea of being Kingsmen, but again she hissed at him, pointing upward. He looked up quickly. Above them was the largest group of caves. One seemed more foreboding than the rest; it had a great, yawning mouth and was dark and silent.

"That'll be old Obit's lair, since it's the biggest and best cave," Reg whispered, stopping below the opening. "If he's returned, we can slip in and I'll . . ." He made a slashing motion with five gleaming claws.

"No, not yet!" Martin softly objected. "We're too outnumbered to start a battle now, and Waymond said only he could fight *him*. For now, let's just try to locate Eric and the captives."

"Hum-harumph," Reg rumbled, pondering the

situation. "Well, then, you two slip in and spy out the lay of the land—the cave, that is." He chuckled. "And snip the sorcerer's beard if you find him," he growled.

"You want us to go in by ourselves?" the children asked almost together, shivering in their wet clothes.

"Shhh," the cat purred. "I'm a warrior, not a spy! And this, you've convinced me, is spy's work for now. I'll stand guard here. That way, you'll have only sundry Sneaks and Snitches, Wraths and Slashes to deal with—if the sorcerer doesn't waken."

Jodi gave Martin a frightened glance and repeated her experimental prayer several times. Looking upward at the dim light from nearby caves, Martin gulped, "But I don't even have my toy sword, much less a real one."

"Stop worrying about what might be," Reg warned. "You made a botch of your chance to remain comfortably out of danger, now didn't you?"

They both nodded abjectly.

"So now you have that second chance you were talking about," Reg stated, staring at them. "Don't worry; the King'll help you."

"But we've never *seen* him," Jodi protested.

Reg laughed softly and pushed them on their way with one paw.

There seemed no other way about it. It was a choice of either going into Obit's den or submitting to the disgrace and fear they had allowed him to bring upon them. Jodi and Martin nodded to each other, and Martin firmly gripped Jodi's hand. Cautiously, they made their way up the cliffside to the looming mouth of the cave. Reg went to stand guard duty in the shadows.

Martin, with Jodi close on his heels, stopped just inside the ominously dark entrance. After several moments of waiting to see if guards were posted inside, they slipped into the throat of the cave. It was like entering a nightmare.

The cave smelled clean, as though Obit would allow no Stenches in his personal quarters. The ceiling was high and the floor was dry. But on the dry, clean floor the squenching of water in their soggy sneakers echoed slightly no matter how quiet they tried to be. In fact, the rough stone walls seemed to make even their heartbeats echo.

Deeper they went, looking here and there. They fully expected a Wrath's screech or a Slash's ax blow at any moment. Frequently they jerked their heads around, anticipating the flash of an ax blade the instant before it whacked off their heads. But nothing happened, and gradually they stopped shivering and took heart.

"Maybe . . . the sorcerer . . . isn't at home," Martin whispered into Jodi's ear in absolutely the softest whisper he could make.

She was about to nod hopefully when they heard faint snoring. They froze. Hearts throbbing, they waited a long while . . . then began to inch forward with their hands stretched out into the darkness.

The rhythmical snoring gradually became louder as they worked their way farther and farther into the dark cave. With their feet they could feel that they were following a deeply worn rut—which meant that many heavy feet regularly had passed that way. Martin worried about meeting the beasts who had made the rut until he realized that the snoring sound was coming from the right side of the tunnel. He groped his way toward the sound and found another passage. It was an oval, smaller tunnel with a low roof. Dim light was coming from the end of it.

Despite the warnings screaming in his head, Martin felt a strong impulse to go into the side passage. On

tiptoe he led Jodi along one wall of it. He quickly
noticed that the floor was smooth, not rutted, and felt
carpeted. He knelt, squinted, and saw a faint pattern
of dragons swirling in a sky battle and foul beasts
contesting one another in a swamp. He stood and
whispered, "The carpet. . . ."

"Shsst!" Jodi warned, pointing toward the room
into which the passage opened. Side-by-side,
scarcely breathing, they crept to the room's entrance.

Peeking in, they saw a candle burning in a twisted
iron candleholder. The candle cast pale, yellow light
over a small, round area of the room. Beside the candle
was an enormous bed, a bed far larger and taller than
any they had ever seen before. It had four posts, one at
each corner; each post was carved in the shape of
twining serpents locked in a death struggle. The bed
was overcovered by a canopy of red material. From the
edges of the canopy hung gold tassles tied, Martin
thought, like scalps. And on the bed, covered by a
blood-red sheet, they saw a solitary figure sleeping. It
was Obit.

In the dim glow, they saw that he was lying perfectly straight. His feet seemed crossed, and his hands
were folded on his breast as though he were protecting himself. Indeed, his face, which was kindly again
in sleep, twitched as though he were having terrible
nightmares. When the children saw that he was deep
in slumber, they advanced slightly into the room.
Then, they halted in terror.

At the foot of the bed, on the carpet, they saw a
sleeping shape, dark and rounded. Cautiously, they
leaned closer and saw that the shape was the foreman
of the Slashes, keeping guard at the foot of his master's bed. The snoring sound was coming from him.
His ax had slipped from his hands and lay on his
rising and falling chest. *Sleeping before another late*

night's work, Martin thought. He swallowed hard and began repeating his prayer to the King.

While Jodi lingered in the passage opening, Martin tiptoed toward the awful bed, fully expecting the restlessly sleeping sorcerer to rise up at any moment and wither him with a spell. But the stiff form did not stir.

Next, Martin imagined that Obit was simply lying in wait, pretending to sleep. As that fantasy flickered through Martin's mind, he found that he could not get his feet to move. Then, he became aware of a warm glow inside himself. He shook his head, smiled, and forced himself forward, his eyes darting from the Slash to the sorcerer.

When he had entered the room, Martin had had no real idea of what he was to do there. But as he went forward he noticed something familiar hanging from the snout of one of the serpents twisting up the bedpost to the left side of the sorcerer's head. The hanging object was nothing less than the Horn of Meet, which Obit gloatingly had shown them back in the Forest clearing. The soft candlelight reflected dully from the silver bands around the horn. Martin checked the sorcerer's breathing and glanced at the Slash to make sure he had not moved. All seemed in order as Martin crept on again.

However, just as he was about to reach up to lift the horn, a prolonged groan rumbled from the Slash. He shifted, and his enormous ax clunked against the floor. Martin felt as though he had turned into a rock, so frozen did he become. The groan stopped, and the Slash merely rolled over in his sleep, no doubt dreaming pleasantly of trees falling and smoke boiling up to fill the sky. Martin felt the glow inside himself brighten, so he took another step toward the horn, looking to his right at the outstretched form of Obit. The old man's face, though twitching, *was* kindly,

Martin saw. Martin could not imagine such a nice-looking old man doing awful things, and the boy suddenly felt pity in his heart for the sorcerer.

But, thought Martin, *he tricked us, so now we must try to correct the matter.* He reached up and lifted the horn off the snake's snout without making a single sound. He turned on his tiptoes and put one foot most carefully in front of the other until he had rejoined Jodi.

She, meanwhile, had watched the sleeping sorcerer and had been tormented by visions of slavery, of dark aloneness, and of the cackling sorcerer controlling her. But as Martin had slipped toward the head of the bed, she had noticed a dark, lumpy object at the feet of the sleeping Slash. It had seemed familiar. A gentle voice in her head had urged her to go stealthily to the object, and she had obeyed. The lumpy thing was Waymond's bag. She had picked it up and was on her way back toward the passage when the Slash had groaned and turned over in his sleep. Though her feet had screamed *"Runrunrun!,"* a warm glow inside her had made her so calm that Martin had not even noticed her until he was by her side.

Now, they stood together at the opening of the passageway, each with a treasure. Without daring to smile at their success, they inched their way out of the dusky chamber. When they reached the main tunnel they stopped to decide what to do next.

"We shouldn't push our luck," Jodi whispered close to Martin's ear.

"We can't leave without trying to rescue Eric and find the captives," Martin quickly whispered back. "Besides, I don't think luck is what's helping us." He turned toward the darker end of the cave and led the way. Reluctantly, she followed close behind him, gripping the leather handles of Waymond's carpetbag in one sweating hand.

Almost at once they smelled a stink that they recognized as belonging to Slashes; it was a mixture of stale smoke, rancid sweat, and putrid breaths. As the children went a hundred yards or so on into the pitch black throat of the cave, the smell became stronger and stronger.

"Must be dozens, maybe hundreds of them ahead," Martin murmured.

For a moment, Jodi closed her eyes in dread. Then she forced her feet forward—one step at a time. As she crept along the worn cavern floor behind her brother, she flinched whenever more sounds of snoring came to them. She began to feel claustrophobia when she sensed the tunnel floor dropping into the earth at a sharp rate . . . yet she kept going. She even kept moving as they slipped past side passageways that led to rooms echoing with the snores of many Slashes. But she, like Martin, froze motionless whenever a grinding groan came forth to startle them. And after each groan it was all she could do to go on after Martin.

They had passed ten or so side passages when they came to a round-topped, stone door set into the right-hand wall. Iron bars were upright in a small window near the top of the door; a large keyhole pierced the door's center. Two Slash guards were sleeping by the door, one on either side; their backs were against the wall, and their thick, hairy legs were outstretched. By their sides lay huge axes whose nicked, stained heads gleamed in the flickering light of one stubby candle. The guttering candle was stuck upon a rock shelf to the left of the door. Jodi and Martin stood for a long while watching the Slash guards to make sure they did not stir, then Martin slipped toward the window. Without making a sound he stood on tiptoe and peered into the cell behind the door.

All he could see, however, was darkness—though a pale glow came from the left of the cell. Slinging the horn around his neck, he reached over the Slash on his left and took hold of the burning candle. He gave it a slight jerk and freed it. Carefully he drew it toward himself, trying not to spill any of the hot wax on the bare chest of the beast sleeping beneath him.

But he trembled just as he was about to get the candle to the door. Two or three drops of the molten wax fell from the candle, and Jodi and Martin caught their breaths as the wax dribbled onto the naked, hairy belly of one of the guards.

"GGnarrr!" it rumbled, rubbing the burned spot with one snaggle-nailed paw. But it did not open its eyes. Evidently, the Slash was exhausted from the labor of felling trees, and so it merely growled as if dreaming that an ember from one of the burnings had scorched it. The beast rolled onto its side and lapsed into deep slumber again—to the very great relief of Martin. He was holding the candle in both hands without so much as batting an eyelash.

Martin's courage—and breathing—soon returned to him, and he lifted the candle up to the barred window of the dungeon. The flickering yellow light flew into the inky darkness, illuminating first the stone walls. Then Martin saw many heavy chains tangled and a group of twenty or so children lying at the ends of the chains on the bare cell floor. Martin's eyes grew wide. Most of the children were awake, looking at the boy's face in the window of their cell.

Martin blinked, surprised that the children did not look unhappy. They were clothed in filthy rags; their bodies were bruised and cut. Their hair was incredibly tangled, and their ankles and wrists were tightly, cruelly manacled. From the manacles to rings in the stone walls ran the heavy, rusted chains. But the watching children all were smiling.

As Martin stared, he saw that some of the children began nodding toward the left of the cell. Craning his neck, Martin looked where they were looking, and he became aware of a light. By pressing his face into the cold bars, he saw that someone else was in the dungeon—someone who was not chained. The free person and the light came noiselessly forward. Suddenly, Martin caught his breath and almost dropped the candle.

The light, Martin saw, was coming from a man—but he was no ordinary man. He was clothed in a soft, white glowing flame! Martin's hand and the candle trembled, so he handed the wax stub to Jodi. Leaning up to the barred window again, without the candlelight in his eyes, Martin saw more clearly the figure robed in white, soft flame. Martin's eyes grew wide and his heartbeat raced; the man was looking at him gently and with a powerful outpouring of love. Martin gave a soft cry and felt as though he were shrinking; his one thought was, *But I don't deserve that kind of love!* Martin began to cry.

Jodi was greatly alarmed, especially when Martin began to cry. "Wh-what's the matter?" she stammered, touching him.

When he turned, his look startled her; she had expected him to look horrified—but his face was joyous. "It's the King!" he cried excitedly, then caught himself and glanced down at the sleeping Slashes. He grabbed her hands and pulled her to the window. "Look!" he commanded in a thrilled tone.

Confused and trembling, Jodi leaned up on the door and peered into the dungeon. She, too, saw the person clothed in soft flame and was pierced by the look

flooding from his eyes. She suddenly felt very warm and had to choke back the tears that were welling up from deep inside her. When she could stand the look no longer, she sagged backward. Martin wrapped his arms around her as she cried silently.

"It's all right," he murmured, reaching up to stroke her hair.

"But, Martin," she whispered, avoiding his look, "I feel so . . . so *dirty!*"

"I know; I did too. But look again. He *knows* us—everything!—and he still loves us more . . . more than . . . oh, I don't know what! Just look."

They wiped their faces, stood on tiptoe, and put their heads close together to look into the dark cell. They saw that the tall, radiant figure standing calmly in the midst of the chained children was gazing at the two wide-eyed faces in the window.

"See?" Martin whispered as his excitement bubbled over. "He forgives us! He forgives us for *everything!*"

Jodi felt her tears flowing freely as she swallowed a sob. Impulsively, she murmured to the King, "I'm sorry . . . I'm so very sorry."

Martin echoed her words, and immediately a feeling of great peace flowed into him. As the King smiled, Martin smiled. "I love you!" Martin spoke quietly into the dungeon.

The King's smile grew—a kind, loving smile that comforted both children more even than cuddling in their mother's lap had ever done. It was then that Jodi and Martin realized that the King was among the captives to comfort them. They saw plainly that it was his presence that enabled the chained children to smile despite their awful situation.

Martin whispered, "I'll bet he could look at even Slashes and old Obit the way he's looking at us."

As tears continued to run down her cheeks, Jodi put her hands to the rusted iron bars. Desperately she wanted to run into the arms of the King. "No wonder the sorcerer hates him so," she murmured to Martin. "He's the most beautiful, loving person I've ever seen."

The King raised one finger to his lips and cautioned them to silence. Then he stretched out one radiantly white arm and pointed in the direction Jodi and Martin had been going—down the tunnel.

"We must hurry and find Waymond—if he's alive—or the Zooks," Jodi whispered, glancing down at the snoring Slash guards.

"Eric first," Martin said quietly.

With her head held high, Jodi nodded, noticing how resolute her little brother had become. She grasped his left hand and squeezed it as they took one last, long look at the King. And looking into the loving eyes of the King gave them the same feeling that looking into the candlelight in the clearing had given them. But the feeling they drew from the King was immeasurably stronger. Martin felt he could now walk boldly through ranks of Slashes. Furthermore, and strangely, he felt he could no longer hate them or any of the other poor slaves of Obit. He and Jodi waved goodbye to the captive children and to the King and left the door of the cell. Martin took the candle and led the way.

Hand in hand, they stealthily walked on down the descending tunnel, straight past more sleeping Slashes. Several times, Jodi felt fear begin to bubble up—but each time it did, the warm glow she had gotten from the King quenched the fear. She smiled as she carefully placed one foot in front of the other one.

In a deserted part of the dank, foul-smelling tunnel, Jodi stopped Martin. Excitedly, she whispered, "Now

I understand why the King doesn't just wipe out Obit and his horrible slaves and free the captives by force! I didn't understand until I saw the look he gave us."

"Right," Martin hurriedly whispered, "because if he were the kind of king who went around wiping out people, he'd be no better than Obit. And he would have killed *us* because for a while *we* were Obit's slaves." He squeezed her hand as they grinned thankfully at each other. "Now come on," he urged. "We've got a job to do."

She shifted Waymond's bag from one hand to the other and followed. Foot by foot, they crept on for another hundred or so yards. Frequently they had to pass gangs of Slashes slumbering along the walls. But neither Jodi nor Martin felt the numbing fear that had so weakened them earlier. Finally, they came to an open room.

Inside the large room a number of the hairy beasts were snoring, sprawled haphazardly on the cold, stone floor. Martin slung the Horn of Meet behind his back and held the candle into the doorway of the chamber. At first, he saw nothing but the Slashes. He started to turn away. But he stopped, having vaguely seen something he thought he recognized. He looked again, holding the candle into the room as he ignored the Slashes sleeping at his feet. There, on the far side beyond thirty or more prone beasts, lay his friend, Eric the Zook! But the boy hunter was very different from when Martin had last seen him.

Martin thought, *How can I get Eric out?* He wondered if he could awaken Eric by throwing a pebble at him. Or by whispering loudly. No, he decided; either way might arouse the Slashes. Martin gulped, looking into the room. It was then that Martin *knew* that, though he couldn't see him, the King was right beside him, offering his hand. Martin smiled and motioned for Jodi to remain on watch in the tunnel. Then, smiling still, he crept into the side cavern.

Slashes lay here and there at random, some with their legs on others' chests, some with their arms crossed. Bodies lay tangled, and gleaming axes were strewn about haphazardly. The cave floor looked as though huge jackstraws had been poured onto it. Picking his way through the mess was no easy task, for Martin had to step over a hairy arm here and a beefy leg there while avoiding axes and gaping-mouthed heads snoring lustily. To make matters worse, he was forced to hop aside frequently when one of the slumbering creatures kicked or shoved one of its fellows that had rolled against it. And each time Martin hopped, he had to hold the candle most carefully to keep hot wax from splattering onto the bare bodies below him.

When he was smack in the middle of the maze, the risk of it all almost overwhelmed him. The stench was terrible and the snoring was awful. Thoughts swarmed through his imagination: *How far away was the hour when the Slashes went to work? Why, in fact, were they still sleeping when usually they worked during the night? And what would they do to him and Jodi if they all awoke?* Then, however, Martin became aware of a warmth, and he realized that the invisible King was standing patiently beside him. He reached out for the King's unseen hand—just in time too, for he was a quarter inch away from stepping on the outflung fingers of one huge beast. Maintaining his balance by leaning on the King's presence, Martin soon stood over his friend.

Eric lay as though he were an empty, discarded, and dirty sack. His head was cradled on one scratched arm, and his bruised legs were drawn up almost to his chest. He was breathing in jerks as though he had been crying. Martin's throat tightened with pity as he bent down, sheltering the candle's flame with one hand. Kneeling close to Eric's upturned ear, he whispered, "Zook, arise."

Eric stirred but did not awaken, so complete was his exhaustion. Martin could see how banged up and scraped his friend was, and he wondered what awful things had been done to him before he was thrown into the chamber. Martin glanced around to make sure none of the Slashes was watching him, then bent over Eric again. "Arise, Zook!" he said, slightly louder this time.

" 'M comin'," Eric mumbled, struggling to awaken.

Martin took his hand away from the flame and gently touched Eric on his left shoulder above one particularly nasty gash. "Zook, arise!" he said almost aloud.

Eric's eyes fluttered open, and for a moment he stared around in terror. Martin quickly clapped his free hand over Eric's mouth before he could cry out, and his friend first looked at him wild-eyed, then smiled and relaxed. Martin took his hand away.

"Martin," Eric whispered. His eyes drifted shut, then opened again. "Oh, am I glad . . . ." Suddenly, he sat up, looking with a broad grin at Martin. "Your face," he murmured, "it's . . . it's . . . you've seen the King, haven't you?" He gripped Martin's shoulders excitedly.

Martin happily nodded.

"No wonder you could get in here without being killed," Eric softly said, stiffly climbing to his feet with his friend's help.

Martin took Eric by one dirt crusted hand and cautiously led him toward the doorway. Eric stumbled once but kept his balance by leaning on Martin's hand. They went on, stepping over beastly arms and legs, feet and faces, until they reached the portal. When Jodi saw Eric, she immediately hugged him. Then she began to cry silently as she brushed dirt from his face and hair; when Eric saw her face his smile came back bigger than before. She could hardly wait to tell him, "We've seen the King! And we know he loves us and is our friend!" Eric started to say something but could not; instead, he hugged Jodi tightly.

As they hurried away from the mass of Slashes and went up the long, damp tunnel, Eric leaned close to whisper, "You don't know how lucky you are! Lots of people never see the King, because they don't look for him, and *lots* more don't even believe he's for real."

Jodi stopped instantly and looked as though she were about to cry. "They need to be told, don't they?"

Eric nodded cheerfully. "That's one of the main things all Zooks are expected to do."

"Speaking of Zooks," Martin began, taking the Horn of Meet from around his neck. He offered it to Eric.

"No; you keep it," Eric muttered, hanging his head as his smile faded. "I failed in my mission and don't deserve to have the horn."

Jodi and Martin exchanged looks, and Martin quickly leaned up to Eric's ear to whisper, "We failed too."

At first Eric looked surprised, but then he nodded and said softly, "No matter; you'll be Zooks proper for all you've done tonight—if we can get out of here."

"Oh, that's no problem," Martin stated confidently. "The King's with us." He led the way with the stubby candle's light.

Holding one hand before the flame, Martin slipped cat-like past the Slashes sleeping along the cavern walls. As silently as three sparks the children quickly arrived at the cell of the captives. A faint white glow was still visible within the dungeon, and Martin pointed to it.

Eric nodded sadly and whispered, "Obit captured them days ago. "He's been torturing them, trying to . . ."

"No," Martin said softly, "you don't understand. Go look inside."

Eric stealthily went to the thick, stone door and put his face to the bars of the window. Martin grinned as he watched his friend become excited and hurry back wide-eyed. "The King!" Eric said almost too loudly. "So that's where you saw him, and that's why the captives haven't given up and become Sneaks!" Suddenly his happy expression faded, and he became sad, "I wish he'd come to me."

"Did you ask him to?" Martin inquired gently.

"Well, no . . . ," Eric answered hesitantly. "I . . . I was afraid he'd be mad at me for . . . for betraying his trust in me."

"Nonsense," Martin snapped, glancing at the Slash guards sleeping on either side of the door. "Go look again."

When Eric came back the second time, tears were trickling down his grimy cheeks. He sniffed twice and wonderingly murmured, "He forgave me." Martin offered him the Horn of Meet, but Eric still refused it. They went on then, more quickly than before but just as quietly.

In a few minutes they came to the passageway that led into the sorcerer's bedchamber. Past it they crept so cautiously that not even the air was disturbed. At the mouth of the cave, Martin threw away the bit of candle, peered outside, and made a soft, purring noise.

"Uh? What?" a drowsy voice mumbled from below.

The children climbed down the cliff and saw Reg. He stretched up and down, back and forth as they gathered around him.

"Some guard you are," Martin chided, petting the cougar's nose.

"Got bored, I did," Reg said sleepily. "Sprung your friend, I see."

"And we found the dungeon where the captive children are," Martin grinned. "But best of all, we got to see the King!"

Reg ha-harumphed and seemed to smile. "Magnificent, isn't he?" he purred.

Martin nodded, then looked at Eric. Eric's eyes were wide, for though he had seen the great warrior cats that roam the Forest, he had never been so close to one. Martin quickly said, "Reg, this is Eric Vanover; Eric, meet Reginald Potterpost Baskenberry. If it suits him, you may call him Reg." Eric nodded slowly, obviously impressed by the cougar's name and size.

"Come on, Martin," Jodi urged. "Let's get away from this terrible place and call the Zooks."

"Right you are," Reg agreed. "Lively, now."

"You're one to talk," Martin teased, following the cougar.

The caves of the Sneaks and Snitches were lightless, but occasionally a moan or a scream echoed from the dark holes, as though some creature inside were having a nightmare. Martin felt sorry for Obit's slaves, but boy! was he glad he now knew the King. As he walked behind Reg, he quickly told Jodi and Eric what he had earlier thought—that they should be called Kingsmen. By the time the group had reached the river blocking their westward journey, Jodi and Eric were as excited about the new name as Martin was.

Reg bounded into the river and swam quickly across. The children followed, holding hands so none of them would be swept away by the strong current. On the other side, Reg plopped down and almost violently began licking his wet fur. When Martin walked past, he chuckled at the warrior cat.

"Two baths in one night are two too many!" Reginald said haughtily as he loped after the children.

They were almost past the mouths of the Snitches and Sneaks' caves when their troubles began anew. They were going up a narrow, winding trail along a cliffside, and Eric, being exhausted and very sore, was not as cautious as he otherwise would have been. He accidentally kicked loose a stone. It was a large stone, and his kick sent it crashing into a whole pile of stones on a ledge below. Those stones crashed to the riverbed with an enormous clatter.

"Whoop, snoop!" a dozen voices cried out from nearby caves. "Alarm and arm, up and shout, trouble's about!" a deep voice bellowed.

"Run for Hopesmont!" Reg called from behind the children. "I'll hold off the beasts!"

The Kingsmen took him at his word and sprinted ahead into the darkness, hoping they did not fall over the many rocks on the steeply rising path. Lights from quickly rekindled fires flared up behind, ahead, and above them. Shouts awakened all the sleeping slaves in the canyons. Forms dark and swift rushed out, stirring a din of crashing rocks. Torches were lit and carried forth in the huge hands of Slashes. The screams of aroused Wraths rent the night. Soon, all Crossingsend was awake and in arms.

Martin sent Jodi ahead as he lingered to help Eric painfully make his way up the trail. They climbed without looking back until they reached the top of the cliff. There, they stopped to catch their breath.

A loud, squalling clamor arose below and behind them. Earsplitting shrieks and wails echoed within the stone walls of the canyon, and in the flaring light of torches they could see more than one gashed body being flung far out into the river's dark water.

"Reginald finally got the battle he wanted," Martin grimly observed, breathing heavily.

"Let's not waste the time he's giving us," Eric panted, looking around to get his bearings. "This way," he called. "To Hopesmont!" He set off to the west, running as fast as he could across the gouged, stump studded ground where smoke hovered thickly.

Behind them came the sounds of furious battle: rending and crashing, wailing and shrieking. But suddenly there was silence. The absence of noise was more chilling to the fleeing children than the clash of warfare. It meant that Reginald had been overcome.

Suddenly, there arose a din of victorious grunts and shouts. The clamor grew louder as the horde behind the children came pouring up and over the top of the cliff, the tracker Sneaks yipping in the fore. The pursuit of the Kingsmen had begun, and fierce it was. As Wraths rose quickly into the hazy sky, Slashes hoisted their axes and torches and began to lope with giant strides. Snitches jostled Sneaks for the lead. And behind them stalked the sorcerer, Obit. He was in no hurry. After all, he gloated, there was no way for the children to escape the final downfall of the Land of the King!

Chapter 10

The Battle of Hopesmont

*A*nyone who has ever played a game of chase knows that when you are running from someone who is close behind you, there's a tingling sensation on your back. It's as though you can actually *feel* a hand reaching to tag you. The sensation makes you suddenly run faster and maybe laugh as you dodge to one side or the other.

Eric, Martin, and Jodi had that feeling as they ran and ran. They, however, were not laughing. They were not making a sound—except for panting and small grunts whenever they stumbled. In the darkness they barely could see one another, much less what they were running into. And all the while it felt as though some lumbering beast was reaching toward their backs with a clawed paw, not to tag them but to knock them down and drag them back to the sorcerer's dungeons. Yet, the children were not afraid.

In the mud created by the heavy rain, across slippery ashes from the burnings, and into smoky darkness they raced without stopping. They dodged jagged stumps and hills of still-glowing embers and great furrows where trees had been dragged. And constantly they could hear the yapping, yelping, screeching, bellowing of pursuing Slashes, Snitches, Sneaks, and Wraths. Even Reeks and Stenches eagerly had arisen to join the chase. If the children had not had a goal and if they had not seen the King, their situation would have been far beyond hope.

Their lungs and throats burned from constantly gulping in the smoky air. Their muscles ached as though they had just finished four games of soccer and had three more games to play. Yet, this was not a game. Moreover, judging by the chorus of infuriated roars behind them, they knew that something much worse than imprisonment would be done to them if they were caught. Listening to the cries of the hundreds of maddened beasts, Martin realized that death would certainly follow capture.

But Eric was so relieved to be free and to have seen the King that he gained strength as he ran. He became more and more like the Zook hunter he had been, or thought he had been, before he was captured. As he raced over the soggy ground, he began to think of the escape as an opportunity to make up for his earlier foolishness. He became determined not to let the pursuing horde seize either him or his friends!

"This way!" he shouted hoarsely, turning a bit to the north. Despite the lack of a trail and the many burnings and gouges, Eric knew where they were. "Come on," he urged Jodi, who had fallen behind. He stopped to help her climb over the carcass of a giant tree that hadn't yet been dragged away, then raced on before her.

The ground began to slope upward, and ahead they could dimly see a dark, towering wall. *The Forest,* thought Martin as sweat ran down his face and stung his eyes. He figured they were coming to the edge of the cut-and-burned area. Eric passed him, running hard, and he redoubled his own efforts. Behind them came the baying of the beastly army—and it was now closing fast.

Just as the escapees were about to enter the cover of the uncut Forest, Eric slowed to wait for Jodi. As he looked back he dimly saw the leaping, bounding black shapes of Sneaks hot on their trail. He also saw the flickering tide of red-orange torch lights weaving among the stumps, flaring into sparks whenever Slashes bumped one another while trying to be the first to catch and devour the children.

Eric sprinted on, glad that the trees at least might provide hiding places should he and his friends be overtaken. He also was glad that dead leaves covered the mud. The leaves were less slippery, and they would make tracking more difficult for the Sneaks. Eric quickly caught Martin and went into the lead again, steering toward the as yet unseen peak of Hopesmont.

They were dodging back and forth among the great trunks when suddenly Eric stopped. Ahead he caught a glimpse of a low, moving body. Then another . . . and another appeared. Martin and Jodi slid up beside him and immediately bent over, gasping for air. Very much out of breath, Martin wheezed, "What . . . is . . . it?"

"Don't know," Eric panted. "Animals maybe. Come on," he said, forcing himself into a run. With groans the other two came after him. Martin was holding the Horn of Meet tightly against his chest as he ran, and Jodi was lugging the magician's bag.

They had gone only another hundred yards when the shadowy animal shapes appeared—almost popped up—right beside them! The children were startled and expected to be knocked down, bitten, or both. But, instead, they saw that three rather large animals with jack-rabbity hind legs were frolicking around them, whimpering.

"Coonets!" Eric laughed. "Sounds as if they're lonely for a friendly face." He reached down and petted the long nose of the nearest animal and briefly stroked its brown and black striped back. The animal gratefully washed his hand with its exceptionally long tongue and wagged its exceptionally long, ringed tail. "Come on if you want to stay alive!" Eric cried to the trio of coonets as he raced on.

As Jodi and Martin ran, they looked sideways at the frisking animals. The children were a bit suspicious of the coonets until they saw quite plainly how glad the creatures were to have found friendly people. "Poor things," Jodi panted. "They probably . . . haven't done anything . . . but run from Slashes and Stenches . . . for days."

Martin tried to nod and run at the same time but almost fell down. He was very, very tired. However, the sudden appearance of the free-spirited animals cheered him. He raced them to keep up with Eric.

Eric soon dropped back, listening for sounds from the Forest as he loped beside Jodi. Together, they wound their way among the tree trunks up the rising ground. "It sounds like . . . ," he dodged a tree, "the beasts have slowed down." He panted, then continued. "I wish we could . . . ," he dodged another tree, "make them think we've gone to . . . Wayshead . . . while we go to Hopesmont."

"I'll lead them off," Martin volunteered, stumbling in his tiredness.

"No, we need to stick together," Eric said, sprinting across a small clearing. "There's some hard ground ahead . . . if I remember correctly. Maybe we can

. . . ," he ducked a low branch, "turn off the trail there and make them think we went on."

"The Sneaks'll smell our trail," Martin objected.

Jodi saw how eager and grateful the coonets were, and quickly an idea formed. "Say," she proposed, "why don't we put something that *smells* like us on the coonets and try to send them toward Wayshead? Surely they can outrun the slaves."

"Good idea!" Eric agreed, slowing. "Better still, let's tie our shoes onto their feet so when the coonets get to muddy ground they'll make tracks like ours. In this darkness, the Sneaks won't know the difference."

"It'll never work," Martin commented wearily.

"Got any other ideas?" Eric inquired.

Martin did not, and as he thought about it and looked at the eager coonets, the idea did not seem so bad. In fact, as he listened to the thunderous yelling-screeching-screaming once more gaining on them, it seemed a very good thing to try.

When they reached the harder ground at the foothills of Hopesmont, they stopped. Quickly they untied and removed their shoes while the coonets clambered all about, licking the children's faces and hands.

"Quit . . . quit!" Martin protested. "I can't see as it is!" The coonet nearest him obeyed; it sat on its haunches, grinning and waiting for the frolic to continue. Martin reached out and grabbed it, and before it could squirm free he had tied his sneakers onto its overlarge hind feet. Jodi and Eric did the same to the other coonets, then stood to see what would happen. At first, the animals just sniffed at the shoes.

"Go to Wayshead," Eric commanded, bending near the coonet that was wearing his footgear. He pointed in the direction of the King's Hall. "Go on. You're fast; you can lead the beasts away from us."

Whether it was the King's charm that lay upon the coonets or whether they simply enjoyed games, they ran off as they were told.

"Now," Eric said, sighing as he looked north toward the black bulk of the peak, "to Hopesmont. And pray our pursuers follow the coonets' trail!"

Barefooted, they cautiously ran up the slopes of the foothills. The rocks hurt their feet, but in the excitement they scarcely noticed. Giant trees soared upward beside them, but gradually the huge trunks were replaced by thick brush—sumac and elderberry, bare fruit trees, and thorny vines. Hearing the beastly army burst from the Forest and storm onto the trail westward, Eric grabbed his companions and turned them toward a thicket of vines. Into the thicket they crawled, stifling yelps as thorns stuck their hands and knees. They crouched and waited breathlessly.

The slaves howled and stormed, screamed and snapped along the trail, not two hundred yards away. The Forest below and south of the children grew bright with the passing of hundreds of flaring torches. The night became filled with the awful sound of beasts tramping along, stepping on one another's heels, pushing and shoving. The flickering orange-red lights and quarrelsome, enraged voices took a long time to go by—so long in fact that Martin and the others were about to burst from holding their breath. Not once, though, did any of the Sneaks or other ugly creatures turn aside from the false scent laid down by the coonets.

"Trusting little creatures," Jodi said quietly of the coonets when the horde had passed. "Hope they don't get caught like Reginald did."

Eric sat up. "Don't worry about the coonets. If they don't want to be seen, they won't be." Squinting into the darkness, he poked gingerly into the thorny vines and began to pluck large blackberries. "Umm!" he mumbled as Martin and Jodi quickly joined him in picking the berries.

"Seems Obit wasn't able to bring fall to all the Forest," Jodi observed, chewing the sweet moisture from the berries.

"Hmm, these are good," Martin slurped.

"The whole Forest was like this once," Eric commented regretfully as he reached to pick more berries. "It was *filled* with fruit trees and all kinds of good things to eat."

A peaceful picture of an abundant Forest was just beginning to form in Jodi and Martin's imaginations when suddenly Eric gripped their arms. They were so startled that they almost cried out . . . but they were glad they hadn't. Shuffling slowly up the slopes of the foothills, a good distance behind his army, came the bent form of Obit. His gray-robed figure was dimly visible near the place where the coonets and children had parted company. Remembering the way the sorcerer had seemed to read her mind, Jodi almost panicked. But Martin took her hand, and she could see that his eyes were closed as he calmly prayed to the King. Instantly, she did likewise.

The stooped figure sniffed here and peered there, working his way closer and closer to the children's hiding place. Luckily, the hoof and paw prints of his army had churned away any tracks or scent . . . and yet he kept coming toward the crouching trio. Their hearts sank even deeper as they felt a breeze come up, blowing the smoke away and letting starlight fall upon the foothill slopes. The bent old man shuffled more rapidly toward them, casting his head left and right.

When he was quite close, they could see his eyes— eyes burning with hatred, eyes of a merciless hunter.

Eric groped cautiously around for a rock to bash him with should he come upon them. But he need not have worried. At the very moment old Obit lifted his head and looked directly toward their thicket, a hoarse shout boomed from the west. The sorcerer turned his head and straightened to listen. Closer now, the deep shout of a returning Slash came again, calling, "Tracks, master . . . *tracks!*" Doubt deepened the frown upon Obit's face, and he seemed undecided. But the Slash seemed so certain that Obit turned and went toward him. In minutes, he had disappeared into the night.

"Phew!" Eric breathed quietly. "That was *close!*" He saw Martin and Jodi grinning at him, then laughed. "I know; I shouldn't have worried. But, like before, I let down my guard and got sloppy. Come on."

Refreshed by the berry break and by the latest evidence of the King's continuing help, the children mustered enough strength to climb the ever-rising slopes of Hopesmont. And a steep climb it was, for foothills soon gave way to upright cliffs. Before long the children had worked their way higher than even the tallest treetops in the Forest below.

As they clambered upward, the moon swung slowly into the clearing sky. From eastward it rose, almost a quarter full and shining with a soft silver light. It lit the mountain and made it seem hoary with age. The moon also gave the children enough light by which to climb. Hand over hand, feet pushing and slipping, legs straining, they helped one another toward the bare rock summit. After an hour or more of effort, they reached it . . . and suddenly they felt completely changed. It was as though they had abruptly become eagles after having suffered like hunted rabbits.

"Ohhh," Jodi breathed as she turned slowly in a

circle to enjoy the unblocked view from the peak. "We're really up high!"

Eric plopped onto a flat rock on the very tip-top. He raised his knees and locked his arms around them as he breathed deeply of the chilly, pure air. To his left, from east to south, lay the broad, slashed area where Obit's slaves had been at work; there hovered the reek of the burnings. About seven miles into that area lay a dark place free of smoke. "That's Crossingsend," he told them, pointing.

"We ran a long way," Martin sighed, lying down so he could rub his sore, stubbed feet. Then he rolled onto one side and looked northward and west where the Forest was a rolling, unbroken ocean of treetops frosted by moonlight. "Look there," he whispered, pointing to the west. They all stood and saw a staggering line of red dots appearing and disappearing under trees.

"They've almost reached Wayshead," Eric noted. "Soon, they'll learn we didn't go that way . . . and then they'll return." He laid both hands on Martin's shoulders. "If you've caught your breath, now is the time to blow the Horn of Meet. And you must blow it for all you are worth!"

"In which direction?" Martin asked, unslinging the arm-long, twisting horn.

"In all directions," Eric told him, holding out one hand as he turned in a circle. "Zooks are everywhere beyond the Great River, waiting for the call."

Martin reverently looked at the Horn of Meet. The moonlight shivered on its silver bindings, faintly illuminating the victory scenes engraved thereon. He took a deep breath and put his lips to the cupped mouthpiece. He blew hard into it . . . but nothing happened except a spewing "Hisss!"

"Buzz your lips and blow harder," Eric instructed.

151

Martin drew a deeper breath and tried again. But only a silly, spitting sound gurgled from the horn.

"Harder!" Eric urged. "Like Joshua before the walls of Jericho!"

Martin took a breath deeper than he would have believed his lungs could hold and pursed his lips. Then he blew.

The sound burst forth louder than several trumpets. It rang and rang until Martin was drained of breath. Even after he let the horn fall to his chest, the sound echoed over the Forest and far away.

"Again!" Eric commanded. "The Zooks are many miles from here."

"Can they come in time?" Jodi asked.

Eric's face was grim. "Zooks can come quickly . . . but who knows? Blow, Martin, as though your life depended upon it . . . because it does."

Martin gulped air into his lungs, then more air . . . and more still. He felt he would burst as he set his lips to the silver mouthpiece. Now that he had the feel of the way to blow it, he knew he could send out an even louder blast. And he did!

The call trumpeted forth so loudly that Eric and Jodi fell away, covering their ears with both hands. So loudly did the call ring out that if there had been walls nearby, they surely would have fallen. For miles and miles the clear, thunderous sound flew. It silenced all the beasts trooping through the Forest and made even the Wraths quiver. Obit, striding along after his army, stopped as though stricken. Quickly, he turned and hastened back toward his lair. And still the call of the Horn of Meet echoed over the Forest and into the lands beyond.

Martin let the horn drop to waist level and gasped for breath. He panted and waited for his hearing to

153

return. "Now what?" he said, nearly shouting since he could hear only a ringing in his ears.

"You must blow it a third time, just to make sure all the Zooks have awakened and are coming," Eric said. "Can you blow it again?"

"I'll try," Martin said softly. He breathed . . . and breathed . . . and breathed, drawing air into his lungs until they were absolutely full. Setting the horn to his lips, he blew the third summoning blast.

Even the trees below and the stars above seemed to tremble from the resounding call. And surely, if you had heard that third call, you too would have grabbed a sword and run to answer it. It was fully five minutes before the echoes of that mighty blast faded into the cool, still distances.

Martin toppled forward, exhausted. Eric caught him and the horn and laid them gently on the ground. "Well done, Martin Zook," he whispered, patting him on one shoulder. "Well done indeed!"

Jodi uncovered her ears and shook her head to clear the ringing. "Now what do we do?" she wondered, taking a seat near Martin.

"We can only wait," Eric replied, also sitting. "And, in the meantime, we must pray the beasts do not overwhelm us here on Hopesmont."

"Shouldn't we go down and hide?" Jodi asked, peering over the edge toward the west. She could see that the ribbon of flickering red dots already had turned around and was retracing its course through the Forest.

"No," Eric stated. "Having declared ourselves, we must remain here—to fight Obit's slaves by ourselves if need be."

"You mean, we can't . . . ?"

"No; no more running or hiding. The battle for the

154

Land will be fought here, on this summit that overlooks it all. And if no one arrives in time, we must perish on this spot!"

There was such authority in Eric's voice that neither Martin nor Jodi dared question him—despite the rapidly approaching line of red torch lights they could see far below in the Forest.

Anxiety, kindled by the waiting, grew upon them like the chill of night. Already, they could sense Murks creeping up the slopes. The children moved closer together, seeking one another's comforting touch. Then, as they touched, they once again felt the King's presence.

"I have a confession to make," Eric said, sitting upright.

"About what?" Jodi asked, thinking of her and Martin's breakfast with Obit.

"About how I was captured."

Martin sat upright, too. "I wondered about that . . . about how a Zook hunter like you could have been taken. Jodi and I were *really* scared when old man Obit showed us your horn after we . . ."

"You told me," Eric interrupted gently. "Anyhow, when Waymond and I left you in the circle, I made my way toward Crossingsend as cautiously as I knew how. As I got closer to it, I began to congratulate myself on having avoided all the gangs of Slashes that were coming to work. I was feeling really fine when I got to the head of Crossingsend's western canyon. Then, I saw it."

"Saw what?" Martin asked, scooting closer.

"A wonderful sword," Eric murmured wistfully, looking off into the distance. "A fine sword, marvelously made. It was lying near my path under the shade of a cedar tree. I thought to myself, *You'd better not go get it; just stick to your task.* But, you know, the sight of that sword pleased me very much. It seemed to be just the sword for me, the 'great' Zook spy and hunter.

"Then a voice came to me, right out of nowhere it seemed. The voice said, 'Eric, you have done well indeed to pass thus far unnoticed. But dangers lie ahead, so you must pick up the sword. After all, you deserve it; such a sword should belong to you!' " He smiled sadly at Martin and Jodi. "I must admit that I was so puffed up by my success that the voice seemed to be speaking the truth. And I thought, *Finders keepers* and things like that. But my heart told me, *Stick to your mission, trust the King, and don't pick up that sword!*"

He looked down at the torch lights, which had reached the foothills at the base of Hopesmont, then quickly resumed his confession. "I wavered, and the voice came to me again. 'What will it hurt?' it asked. 'Just go and pick it up.' When I still hesitated, the voice said to me, 'The King's not around to help you, is he? And you've always wanted to be so strong that no one could harm you. With that sword, you can conquer anything! Just pick it up and see.' So, at last, I did."

Jodi and Martin both groaned, regretfully remembering how they had stepped out of the magic circle to take food from Obit.

"No sooner did I have the sword in my hand than I found I could neither move nor let go of the thing," Eric went on. "Suddenly, Obit appeared, and with him was a gang of Slashes armed with axes. Feeling very angry, I tried to attack them with the sword. But, you know what? It turned into ashes in my hand. All that shining steel simply drifted away like a dream.

The Slashes grabbed me, dragged me down into the canyons, tormented me, and threw me into the chamber where you found me." He sighed, his head downcast.

"But Eric," Martin gently reminded him, "you said the King forgave you."

Eric lifted his head and slowly began to smile.

"And you got us safely here," Jodi added, feeling a growing warmth toward their friend since he had shared his story with them. "Plus, you showed Martin how to blow the Horn of Meet."

Eric's smile widened briefly; then his look became grim. He pointed downward.

Below, flowing upward over the foothills, was a tide of beasts. Their torches lit their fanged faces blood red. In their hands were axes, and in their eyes was fury. Rapidly they climbed the mountain.

The children scrambled to their feet. Eric went to the edge of the summit and glared downward. "In the name of the King, advance no further!" he yelled.

Jodi was thrilled by Eric's brave, commanding tone. And, for a moment, the horde below hesitated, wondering what power stood atop the mountain to challenge them so. But the Slash foreman guffawed. "Aw," he sneered, "there's only them three kids! Let's go eat 'em, boys!"

A grunted chant much like the song they had sung earlier burst out among the Slashes. On they climbed, making an awful racket with their chant as they shook gleaming axes into the red torch light. The beasts who lacked axes picked up stones with which to bash in the children's heads when they got to the top. Stenches, Reeks, Snitches, and Sneaks all scrambled and drifted past and around one another. They chuckled and snickered among themselves, for they believed that if they captured the summit of Hopesmont and crushed the Horn of Meet, their master's victory would be complete.

At that very moment, however, a new sound cut through the chant and laughter. At first a few, then all the beasts stopped, fell silent, and turned toward the new sound. It rang clearly through the Forest. It was a sound of marching feet and high, clear voices singing. The Slashes looked at the Snitches; the Sneaks wrinkled their grimy faces and nervously picked their noses as they stared at the larger beasts for reassurance. But they and all the beastly horde ringing the mountain kept silent as the words being sung came clearly to them:

Marching Song of the Zooks

O! the Zooks come marching,
marching to the fore!
With our swords o'er arching,
ever, ever more!

When the call comes ringing
that some evil's near,
then the Zooks come singing,
singing without fear!

When the need is clear
and a threat's at hand,
then will we appear
with our joyful band!

O! the Zooks come marching,
marching to the fore!
With our swords o'er arching,
ever, ever more!

Jodi, Eric, and Martin joyously jumped up and began to cheer. Standing straight up on the summit of

Hopesmont, they looked out in all directions at many, many upraised shields and swords flashing in the moonlight. Through the Forest of Always the Zooks came marching, singing strongly and without fear in their voices.

The beastly horde below the summit grumbled and turned uncertainly this way and that, not knowing what to do. Their master had not prepared them to face an opposing army, and now he was nowhere to be seen. Darkness and stealth, mud and ashes, fear and foment were the slaves' way—not open battle!

Soon the slaves of Obit found themselves being surrounded by Zooks—Zook girls and Zook boys, all clad in shining armor, all holding round shields and straight swords flashing in the silvery moonlight. And all obviously were determined to drive evil from the Land of their King. Yet few of the Zooks looked older than Jodi or taller than Eric. So great were their numbers and so stout was their resolve, however, that Obit's slaves cowered as they were encircled by the youthful army.

But the head Slash had not been given his position for reasons of cowardice. "To the top, boys!" he roared. "We'll not fall without a fight! Bite 'em and claw 'em, gouge 'em and gnaw 'em!" he bellowed as he led the way up the cliffs. The Snitches and Sneaks, Stenches and Reeks, Murks and Wraths all saw that the mountaintop would be a good place for a last-ditch fight, so they followed the huge foreman upward, clamoring and shrieking. Jodi and the boys began frantically gathering rocks with which to repell the assault.

Before they could hurl a stone, however, out of the Forest and straight through the midst of the beastly army leaped a figure that apparently had been leading the Zooks to war. That figure shoved aside Slashes that rose up in his path and threw down Stenches that tried to trip him. Straight toward the soaring peak of Hopesmont the figure dashed, springing lightly up the steep cliffs. In moments he stood beside the three defenders of the summit.

"Waymond!" Jodi cried, rushing to hug the magician. "We were afraid you'd been killed!"

"My bag," he said, beaming. "Have you got my bag?"

Jodi reached down, grasped the leather handles, and held the carpetbag toward him. While he levelled his carved staff at the slave army below, he turned and said, "Reach into the bag and use what you find to help me fight off this mob!"

Thrilled by the opportunity to delve into the magician's bag of tricks, the three children gladly dug into its depths. Meanwhile, something very startling began to happen.

From the tip of Waymond's staff yellow lightning flashed forth. The blazing shafts of light grew and grew in force and brilliance until they became a glowing outpouring like sunlight. The mountainsides and Forest below soon were illuminated as though day had come. The besieging army of slaves momentarily was blinded. They cowered and fell back. But they could not flee because the Zooks held them within a ring of thrusting shields and threatening swords.

"Onward, beasts!" the Slash foreman cried, raising his dreadful ax. He and the bravest of his fellows began climbing the cliffs again.

Jodi, Martin, and Eric found a number of round balls in the bag. These they took out and began throwing down at the climbing Slashes. When each ball struck, it burst into rainbow colored lightning and billowing white smoke. Stricken Slashes were completely discombobulated.

"Hey, this is fun!" Martin shouted as he hurled a sphere at the Slash foreman. Smack! it hit him squarely on the snout and burst into lightning red, yellow, green, and blue and covered him with a cloud of white smoke. Dazzled and dumbfounded, the Foreman staggered back down the mountain.

In minutes the Battle of Hopesmont was finished. The Reeks and Stenches could not stand the light, nor could the Murks and Snitches. All the Slashes soon were disarmed by brave Zooks who rushed forward. The Wraths were enveloped by the yellow light from Waymond's staff and turned instantly back into the small, gray eagles from which they had been formed. They flew away thankfully. The Sneaks simply fell into curled balls, whimpering at the feet of Zooks who stood over them.

As a strong southerly wind blew the smoke of battle from the mountain slopes, Eric and Jodi were first to notice that the sky's light was not only from Waymond's lightning. The dawn itself was rapidly flowing in from the east. Soon, the sun appeared, smiling over the horizon. Seeing it, the slave horde completely quit, knowing their night of evil had ended.

As the dawn's light poured over him, Waymond stood tall on the summit. "Well done, Zooks!" he cried down, then turned to wink at Martin, Jodi, and Eric. "Well done, Zooks all!" He turned back to the armed and armored children below. "Now, take the Slashes and stand each of them on a stump in the cut-and-burned area! Hold all the Sneaks for later!" He watched as the Zooks marched their prisoners down into the destroyed part of the Forest. Then he said to the trio of Hopesmont's defenders, "As soon as the wind blows the smoke away and the Slashes are all in place, you'll see more of the King's magic."

"What about the Stenches, Reeks, Murks, and Snitches?" Martin asked.

"Oh, they'll return to being harmless bad smells, rustling sounds, shadows, and shaggy moss that are in every forest—harmless until some evil power comes to stir them up," Waymond said, laughing merrily. He began whistling as he climbed down the mountain, swinging his staff. The children happily followed him.

It was as he said: When the sun rose higher in the clearing sky, the Snitches faded into the Forest and became shaggy, gray moss on dark branches. The Murks disappeared—shadows banished by the light. The Stenches and Reeks dissolved and were blown away by the fresh south wind. Soon, all the dreadful things Obit had aroused were gone—except the Slashes and Sneaks.

Prodded by sharp sword points and pushed by sturdy shields, the huge beasts were herded into the cut-and-burned area. Each was made to stand upon a stump, guarded there by a Zook. The hairy creatures were pushed along far and wide until almost all the stumps were covered—not by a gloriously spreading tree, but by the beefy body of a Slash. They did not at all like their treatment, but they had little choice—except, of course, to be cut down by one of the grim-faced Zooks. Furthermore, the sunlight had sapped the Slashes' fearsome strength, so they went quietly until all of them were stationed on jagged, splintered stumps.

Waymond and the trio of mountaintop defenders went to stand near the center of the slashed area. Waymond lifted his staff and turned in a circle, his head thrown back so the warm sunlight shone upon his curly brown beard. The children held their breath in anticipation, knowing he was about to call down some very powerful spell. They watched intently as he concentrated all his attention upon the sky. When at last he spoke, this is what he said:

> *From living roots*
> *and ground so torn,*
> *from stumps and shoots,*
> *let life be born!*
>
> *From them that cut*
> *and them that hewed,*
> *let wrong be shut*
> *and trees renewed!*

The sky grew immensely brighter as the Slashes cringed atop their stumps. Powerful light flowed from the sky and seemed to rise from the ground. The air was soon filled with a warm yellow glow so bright that all the children were forced to shut their eyes tightly.

When they opened them the first thing they became aware of was shade—cool, restful shade. Next, they noticed a whispering melody: the southerly breeze caressing many leaves. Finally, they heard the delightful songs of birds that quickly had returned with the wind. And when they looked all around, they discovered that the Forest had been restored. All the Slashes had been changed into trees . . . not as grand and mighty as the original ones, but growing and green nevertheless.

As the Zooks came together, they pushed the hundred or so Sneaks into a group in the middle of the army. Meanwhile, Waymond rested. Leaning on his staff, he smiled as he listened to the birds singing. Jodi and Martin went to him, and Martin cleared his throat. "Um, sir, I don't mean to push . . . but remember the captives?"

Jodi added, "They're chained in a dungeon in Obit's cave."

"Oh, yes," Waymond said, rousing himself. He straightened and grew serious. "We'd best hurry, hadn't we?" He stood on tiptoe and called instructions to the Zooks. Squads formed, each with its officer. Waymond sent Eric to lead one of the squads.

Then the magician held up his staff. To Martin and Jodi he said, "Lead on, Kingsmen." He nodded knowingly when they looked surprised. "To Crossingsend!"

With that the Zooks slung their shields on their backs, formed their column, and began marching rapidly. The tramp of feet grew loud in the reborn Forest. Waymond smiled and motioned encouragingly to his fellow leaders. Martin took his meaning, turned, and called out, "Onward, Zooks!"

The marching song at once rang out from hundreds of clear, strong voices:

> *O! the Zooks come marching,*
> *marching to the fore!*
> *With our swords o'er arching,*
> *ever, ever more!*

Chapter 11

Breaking the Bane

*J*odi and Martin felt very happy as they marched beside Waymond with the Zooks through the Forest toward Crossingsend. They were delighted to be a part of the great company of bold girls and boys who, with Waymond's help, had won the day and were marching in victory toward the final battle. And yet, two things were bothering the brother and sister. First, they were bothered by the memory of their betrayal of Waymond. And second, they were bothered by the fact that their betrayal, and their dirty bodies, made them feel like Sneaks. They knew that, even though the King had forgiven them, they had to make their peace with the magician.

As they hurried alongside Waymond, they both began to frown. "Uh, sir," Martin began, clearing his throat. "That was wonderful magic you did to the Slashes. I'm glad you didn't kill them."

Waymond nodded, looking at the two children with one eyebrow lifted. "Yes, everyone deserves a second chance, don't they? Even you and Jodi."

"Yes sir," both children hastily agreed.

"I'm glad you know the King has forgiven you," Waymond smiled.

Jodi nodded, then asked, "What about you, sir? Will you forgive us for disobeying you?"

"Yes," Waymond said. His brown eyes sparkled as he added, "But please try not to disobey again."

Both children felt relieved, and Martin said, "I'm glad you're not mad at us, because I was beginning to feel like . . . like a Sneak." He looked back at the gang of Sneaks being herded along in the middle of the Zook column. Suddenly, he felt sympathy for them, especially the ones who looked frightened. "What will be done to them?"

"What would *you* do with them?" Waymond asked, lifting one eyebrow again.

Jodi and Martin frowned thoughtfully, watching the Sneaks. Some were pushing and shoving one another and bickering among themselves even while under guard. Others, however, just looked scared and defeated. Jodi felt sorry for the beaten-looking ones who shuffled along as though no hope existed.

"Some of them act like brats," Martin observed. "But the rest look . . . well, pitiful. What are Sneaks?"

The magician's expression became solemn." They are children who accepted food from Obit."

Martin choked and frowned deeper. "Accepted food?" he repeated in a small voice.

"Yes; like you and Jodi did," Waymond said calmly.

Martin became defensive. "But weren't they simply hungry?"

"Frog flutes and toad trumpets!" Waymond snapped. "There is hunger . . . and there is *hunger*. Sometimes it is better to go hungry for a while than to take food that never truly can satisfy you." He gazed ahead again and soon began whistling a happy tune while Martin and Jodi thought.

After a while, Jodi rather lamely said, "But sir, there seemed to be nothing wrong . . . I mean. . . ."

"I know what you mean," Waymond sighed. "Tell me, though, in your heart of hearts, did you feel it was right to leave the circle?" His gaze settled on Martin.

Martin hesitated; he thought of a great many excuses he could make, but at last he swallowed his pride. "To tell you the truth, sir, I didn't listen to my heart. I simply saw the food and wanted it."

Waymond made no sign of either approval or disapproval. He only kept walking, weaving his way around the thick trunks of the towering trees. He resumed whistling his happy tune.

Martin regathered his courage and tugged on the magician's sleeve. "Sir? About the Sneaks," he began. "I . . . that is, could they be turned back into children?"

"They must first see how dirty they are; then they must *want* to be clean again."

"But sir, you said everyone deserves a second chance. You can't just cast them off!" Martin protested.

"They've cast themselves off, Martin," Waymond said sternly. "They've *chosen* to do bad."

"All of them?" Martin inquired, glancing at the Sneaks. "Yes, some of them act mean. But the others just look scared. What if the Sneaks never had anyone to tell them, or show them, how to act right? What if they grew up with parents who were always angry and unhappy and with friends who were always fighting and unsatisfied? Shouldn't someone at least try to talk to them the way you talked to us?"

"I have no use for children who don't *want* to be brave," Waymond said impatiently.

"That's *you*, sir," Martin said meekly. "What about the King?"

167

"What about him?" Waymond asked, growing angry. "Those Sneaks turned against him. They've done their best to hurt him!"

Martin winced, afraid to make Waymond madder. But he looked again at the Sneaks, and he felt he had to do something about the ones who did not show defiance and hatred. "Sir?" Martin asked quietly. "Couldn't we please go talk to them? Someone has to let them know they don't have to serve a master who'll cause them pain."

"All right. Let's go talk to them," Waymond said, coming to a stop. The Zooks went past until Waymond, Martin, and Jodi were with the gang of Sneaks. Then, Waymond looked at the filthy, defeated creatures with a gaze that Martin thought was hypnotic.

"Tell me truthfully," Waymond asked one urchin, "why did you choose not to follow the King?"

The brat picked at his messy nose and frowned. " 'Cause Obit said he's a sissy. I don't follow no sissy!"

"See?" Waymond quietly asked Jodi and Martin. Martin nodded to another of the Sneaks, and Waymond asked her, "What about you?"

"I heard the King was mean," the girl replied shyly, "and made bad children fall into a lake of fire that burned them forever."

Waymond frowned. "Who told you that?"

"A friend," she whispered, hanging her dirty head and dragging her feet.

"Some friend," Waymond muttered. He turned to others of the Sneaks. "What about you? Why did you choose Obit over the King?"

"The king, sir?" one boy asked, holding the blackened pieces of his shirt together. "What king?"

"Yeah," another chimed. "What's he king of?"

Waymond blinked, surprised. "Why, he's the King of this Land, for one thing. Surely you've heard of him!"

"No, sir," several voices muttered together.

One frightened, filthy girl with brown, curly hair tugged on the magician's sleeve. "Sir, is this king nice? Could I meet him?"

Waymond stared at her, and Martin saw tears spring into his eyes. Speechlessly, the magician led Martin and Jodi to the head of the column. There, he strode along, lost in thought.

Martin finally ventured to ask, "Do you see, sir? What if you'd never *known* the King or had trustworthy news about him? What if you'd never felt the King's forgiveness and love?"

Waymond's head jerked back, and tears brimmed on his lower lids. "I . . . I've never thought about that," he admitted, slowing his pace. He turned his face away from Martin to wipe his cheeks and walked in silence for a while. When he spoke again it was very sadly. "I've always sought the good children, the ones who wanted to be brave. What if I also had sought the others, the ones who were afraid? What if I had brought them to the King and shown them his love?" He began to cry.

Martin reached up and patted his back. "Don't cry," Martin whispered. "Surely the King will know how to put matters right."

Waymond's face brightened by degrees. "Of course he will!" he said, patting the boy's head. Then he grinned with sparkling eyes. "Martin, I like you!"

"I like you, too, sir," Martin smiled, feeling the warm sunshine on his face, "especially because you led us toward the King."

Waymond lifted his head, put one hand on Martin's left shoulder, and stared ahead. Martin sighed, contented . . . except for one small matter that still puzzled him. "By the way, sir," Martin began, "how did you and the Zooks manage to come so quickly to Hopesmont?"

Waymond stroked his beard, looked down at Martin, and winked. "It's no great mystery. When I left you and Jodi in the circle of love, I went to Hopesmont, then to Wayshead. The Hall of the King had been burned, and the valley was occupied by a number of Obit's slaves. I marched right in to scatter them, but," he laughed self-consciously, "I was ambushed. Before I could lift my staff, I was swarmed over by Slashes and Stenches. During the hand-to-hand combat, a Wrath swooped down and snatched up my bag. I freed myself and scorched at least a hundred of the beasts, but by then the Wrath had disappeared with my bag. Obviously, it carried the bag to old Obit.

"Anyway, I routed the remaining slaves of darkness and saw that the captives were not to be found in the valley. About that time, Jodi's eagle came and told me the news of your capture. So, I summoned jays from the southlands and sent them far and wide to gather the Zooks. I then hastened to your rescue. Most of the Zooks already had crossed the Great River and were well into the Forest when your call came echoing over the Land." He smiled broadly. "And a magnificent call it was, I might add." He tousled Martin's hair playfully and laid one hand on the boy's left shoulder. He and Martin looked ahead.

There, the Forest trees were becoming fewer and farther apart. Between them, Martin could see a great, black gash opening up in the Land. He felt Waymond's grip on his shoulder tighten.

"Well," Waymond said grimly, "this is it: Crossingsend and the final battle."

170

As the Zook army and the Sneaks came upon the first of the canyons of Crossingsend, the marching song stopped. Only the tramp-tramp-tramp of slowing feet and the rattle of shields being unslung could be heard. Scouts ran ahead to find trails down into the network of deep clefts in the earth.

When the scouts returned, the magician motioned with his staff for the army to divide into two groups. Silently, the Zooks did so. Then they drew their swords and began the descent. Hearts beat fast, for they had no idea what ambush the sorcerer might have prepared. Jodi stayed close to Eric and let him hold her hand to help her down the steeper parts of the trail. When they reached the bottom, she smiled at him; he grinned back before hurrying to lead the squad to which he earlier had been assigned.

The two winding columns of the army filed down both sides of the westernmost canyon. They trailed along the rocky riverbanks toward the center of the star-shaped valley. To their surprise, no beasts sprang out at them from the open mouthed caves or unleashed avalanches of rock upon their heads. "Where is Obit?" many of the Zooks whispered.

Most of the Sneaks became quite fearful and silent, dreading recapture and reenslavement. They lagged behind the Zooks, not with hopes of escape but in horror of facing their master Obit. The Zooks kept them close together, however, as they made their way around huge red boulders and passed beneath the steep cliffs.

At last the heads of the columns reached the meeting point of the canyons and rivers. There, the army gathered before the ominously gaping mouth of the sorcerer's cave. Waymond stood surveying the troops until they all were assembled. Then he shaded his eyes to look at the cave that Obit had used, as well as at

the surrounding caves. Eric came up with his squad,
and Waymond squinted at him. It was then that the
magician suddenly saw what had been amiss when he
first crossed the Great River with Eric.

"Where's your armor, Zook lieutenant?" Waymond
asked sternly. "And your shield and sword?"

"I . . . I left them at home," Eric admitted. He
glanced ashamedly at Jodi, who had come up behind
him.

"Oh, pillbug pinches!" Waymond snapped. "I
knew there was something not right about you that
night we entered the Land . . . but, preoccupation
and expectation!, I thought you were like Jodi and
Martin." He frowned, then shrugged. "Well, it can't
be helped now. Let someone else lead your squad."

Eric came smartly to attention. "I won't leave my
sword and armor behind ever again," he promised.

"No, I don't imagine you will—not after being captured because you abandoned them!" Waymond
scolded, turning away. Then, however, he seemed to
regret his harsh words. He relaxed and smiled at the
downcast, dirty, and barefoot Eric. The magician laid
his right hand on Eric's shoulders and lifted the boy's
chin with his left hand. "It's all right; only you suffered for . . . well, anyhow, I'm sorry I spoke sharply
to you."

Eric straightened and smiled. "It's okay, sir."

Waymond nodded and pointed with his staff toward the black entrance of the largest cave. Loudly he
said, "Remain here, Zooks. Prepare for combat. I will
go see if Obit is denned up in there."

"That's where the captives are," Jodi told him.

The magician smiled as though to thank her for the
information. "I'll also see to freeing them," he said,
then lost his smile, "if they're still alive."

He drew himself up to his full height and strode

toward Obit's cave. Jodi took one of Eric's hands and gently squeezed it as they watched their guide and friend go toward the task they knew he long had dreaded. Then Jodi remembered. . . .

"What's this about your armor?" she whispered to Eric, watching the magician.

Eric quietly replied, "I'm afraid I . . . uh, got a little cocky after the last adventure. When I returned home, I took off my armor."

Jodi stifled a laugh. "It would look strange, walking around in . . ."

Eric frowned seriously at her. "You don't understand." He glanced up to watch the magician climbing the cliff to enter the yawning cave mouth. Eric continued, "The armor of the King, the armor Zooks wear, becomes invisible whenever you leave the Land. It reappears when you come back across the Great River. Anyhow, since I had no armor, Obit was able to tempt and capture me." He hung his head. "I wasn't as strong as I thought I was," he admitted in a hushed voice.

Jodi squeezed his hand reassuringly, looking toward the shadowed mouth of the cave.

Stillness, broken only by the flowing of the rivers, reigned in the canyons. Wrens and sparrows had returned to their homes, but they were hidden; even they tensely awaited the outcome of the battle between the sorcerer and the magician. The Zooks stood with their shields before them, their feet braced, their expressions grim. Their armor and sharp-edged swords flashed brightly in the sun.

Without prelude, a light brighter than the sunlight burst from the mouth of the sorcerer's cave. The Zooks turned away as the outflashing brilliance flooded over them. The light was followed by the zinging of giant sparks and an outrushing of white smoke. The noise was like that of high voltage power lines slashing across one another during a storm. ZZZIINNGGG! SSSNNAARRRZZZZ! ZZZRRAACCKKK!! Lights of many colors flashed forth, flickering over the rivers and scattering even the far-away canyon shadows. Birds took flight, and the Zooks backed away. Smoke continued to billow out of the cave mouth in great clouds. Rocks tumbled from the cliff above the cave, and the cliff itself was visibly shaken by a widespread trembling. Jodi and several others gasped, fearing that the cave would collapse on the magician and the captive children. But soon the trembling and the sounds stopped. The smoke trickled forth for several minutes more and was blown away by the southerly breeze.

When the last loosened rocks had bounced down the cliff above the cave, a small, dingy figure appeared. It was a child, blinking in the sunlight. Then, another and another dirty, mistreated-looking child appeared until twenty or so were scrambling down from the blackened opening of the cave. Some were limping badly and had to be helped along by their companions. Quickly, the Zooks began to cheer as they rushed forward to help the released prisoners.

As Jodi and others began to ask, "Where's Waymond?" the magician came from the cave. He looked exhausted, older, and bent as he leaned on his charred staff. He stood in the cave mouth for a moment, breathing deeply, then climbed carefully down and made his way across the rocks. A squad of Zooks rushed forward to help him. As he came closer, all could see the immense tiredness in his sunken eyes.

"Did you kill him?" someone ran up and asked the magician.

Waymond slowly shook his head and weakly said, "I did nothing more than obey my King." He turned to point with his blackened staff toward the cave. The children all looked where he pointed. At first they saw only wisps of smoke curling up from the top of the opening to be snatched away by the breeze. Then, from the floor of the entrance, a head appeared—a ghastly head atop a long, snake's body. From the head a bright red tongue flicked in and out, tasting the air to see if the outside world was safe. When the creature had come into the sunlight, it cringed and seemed unwilling to crawl further.

Waymond drew himself upright, standing free of the supporting arms of the Zooks. He levelled his staff at the lingering snake. "Out!" he commanded. "Out and begone, in the name of the King!"

The long, dark brown and green snake ducked back at the sound of Waymond's words, but it quickly reappeared. It slithered down the face of the cliff. Martin and several Zooks edged forward. They saw that the snake was bruised and bleeding and that its diamond-patterned skin was torn as though it had been rolled against rough rocks.

Martin moved even closer as the snake writhed painfully across the rocky canyon floor. It blinked heavy-lidded eyes and rose up slightly in front as it slithered ahead in a sideways fashion. Martin's heart was touched by the wounds and beaten look of the creature. "Poor thing," he murmured.

The snake paused and stared at Martin. Its crimson tongue flicked rapidly as though it were tasting the mercy that was so obvious in Martin's gaze. For a moment, it seemed that the snake might go to the boy in a friendly manner—but then it bared its fangs, hissed, and turned away. Quickly, it swam across a river and crawled into the canyon that led north. In minutes, the children had lost sight of it. Martin regretfully went back to Jodi and Eric.

"But where's the King?" one of the ex-captives asked, sitting by the river. "He was with us until a little while ago."

Heads by the dozen turned this way and that, all searching for even a glimpse of the one they loved more than any other. Then an older Zook shouted, "There! Look there!"

The rest of the Zooks, the ex-captives, and even the Sneaks looked skyward where the boy was pointing. But they were dazzled by the sunlight, which suddenly seemed to grow immensely stronger. When they were able to open their eyes, they saw that a figure clothed in white flame was standing among them.

"A Abba seimt!" Waymond exclaimed in a strange language.

At once the children recognized the King. A cheer burst forth and rang against the cliffs; the words, "Hail to the King! Hail to the King!" filled the canyons and echoed louder than the rushing rivers' roar.

He began to walk slowly among the faithful Zooks. Heads were bowed and swords sheathed as the King went from one youthful soldier to the next. He touched their heads and smiled the kindest, most loving smile Jodi and the open-mouthed Martin had ever seen. When the King came to Martin, he placed his right hand on the boy's head. Martin was filled with pleasant warmth and no longer felt like a bruised, dirty boy with bare feet and stubbed toes. He felt fully like a Zook, a Kingsman of proud bearing and willing heart. Bright-eyed, Martin watched the King turn to look at the Sneaks. He listened closely as the King spoke to the ex-children.

"Slaves of darkness," the King said gently, spreading his arms and hands wide apart to include all the grimy servants of Obit, "what you once were, you may choose to become again. Those who will, follow me." He led the way to the river, stepped out into it so the current swirled around his white robe, and smiled to the Sneaks. Some followed his example quickly, hurrying into the water to wash the dirt and grime from their bodies and matted hair. The King also beckoned to the ex-captives, and they raced into the river and began bathing themselves. The King went to each of the children with him and gently helped them wash their hair and clean the dirt and filth of captivity from their faces and eyes. The clear green current quickly carried the grime away.

The Sneaks who had remained on the shore watched mistrustfully. They frowned as the Sneaks who had gone into the river began to laugh and talk happily while they scrubbed and splashed one another. Children fresh and clean and healed of their wounds emerged from beneath layers of dirt and soot. When the Sneaks on the bank saw that the ones in the water were being restored and actually were having fun, most hurried to join in. A few, however, did not seem to understand what was happening. They refused the King's invitation and began to shrink away from the river.

"Come," the King said, beckoning to them with a graceful motion of his right hand, "join us."

But the few Sneaks remaining on the shore frowned all the deeper and snarled, apparently angered by his friendly words. When his kind eyes settled upon them, they lifted the blackened tatters of their clothing and hid their faces from his sight.

"Please join us," the King repeated, smiling in such a way that Jodi and Martin instantly were drawn toward him. But they realized that something important must first be done. The brother and sister quietly went toward the Sneaks who cowered nearby.

Those Sneaks stood with their backs to the river, snarling at their Zook guards as Martin and Jodi came up to them. They touched first one, then another of the filthy ex-children. It did not offend either Jodi or Martin that the Sneaks drew back suspiciously. "It's all right," Martin assured the cringing creatures. "The King won't hurt you. He just wants you to be with him. Come on, and you'll see that it's okay." Martin smiled in a friendly way, gazing at the Sneaks with blue eyes that frequently had melted the hearts of women and girls he had met. When Jodi also smiled, three, then four, then five of the Sneaks could not resist. They went with Martin and Jodi to the river, holding hands because of fear. "Come on," Martin encouraged them. "I know you don't understand, but really, once you get started, the hardest part's done." Jodi and Martin, walking in a line with the five Sneaks, waded out into the swirling water. And the happiest moment of all their lives was when the King came and helped them wash themselves clean.

The remainder of the Sneaks, however, were not at all convinced that the King meant them no harm. All at once they turned and ran at the Zooks who were guarding them. Shields instantly were thrust forward to stop the Sneaks, but Waymond called out, "Let them follow the master of their choice!"

Sadly, the King and the Zooks watched the Sneaks scurry down the northern canyon after the vanished snake. Martin looked at Waymond, and he saw that the magician's jaw was firm and his eyes were tear-lined. Martin felt certain that from then on the magician would work doubly hard to keep fearful, unloved children from falling prey to sorcerers.

Clean, and pressing water from their hair, the ex-Sneaks, ex-captives, and Jodi and Martin began wading to the bank of the river. The King lifted them with love onto the shore. Jodi and the others immediately noticed that the clothing of the former Sneaks and captives was no longer the poor filthy rags they had been wearing. The restored children now wore new garments—garments of soft, fresh green material. Jodi glanced quickly at Martin, then down at herself. They, too, were dressed in soft, new clothes! She felt so thrilled that she wanted to rush home and begin telling everyone about the King! She was so happy, in fact, that she was among the first to go up to the King and say, "I love you!" The words soon became a resounding cheer.

When the children's voices again were still, one of the ex-Sneaks shyly approached the King. "Please, sir," he said softly, "could we have our names back now? Obit took them, you know."

The King looked around at the cleansed ex-Sneaks, all of whom were expectantly awaiting his answer. He smiled when he saw the look in their eyes. "Yes," he said gently. "You may have your names back—or you may choose new names." He nodded to the boy who had asked the question. "What would you now be called?"

"Me, sir?" the boy asked, pointing to himself. "Why, I'll be Shannon!"

The King nodded. "And you?" he asked a girl near his side.

She seemed to have forgotten her voice until the King touched the crown of her head. "I'm called Rachael, m'lord," she whispered, then suddenly began crying. "Rachael Saenz," she murmured.

So it went, on around the group of reclaimed children. The King walked among them, touching each as he or she spoke a name that meant either a return to childhood or a new life. While the children were speaking their names, Jodi felt aglow with the feeling she had gotten from being washed in the river. Quickly, she found Eric, took his hand, and held it as he grinned at her.

The King slowly went through the army of Zooks, touching them. When he reached the last one, he turned and lifted his right hand. "To Wayshead!" he called, beckoning as he led the way out of the canyons of shadow. Waymond and the children hastened to follow.

"Onward to the Hall of the King!" someone shouted.

"Up with the marching song!" another cried.

At once the song began. It rang cheerily throughout the long, narrow canyons and echoed from the stone walls. Possibly the snake Obit and his Sneaks heard it, but if they did it only made them hurry away faster. Undoubtedly they ground their teeth and snarled at one another in anticipation of returning another time to fight again.

However, for now the Bane was broken, and the army of Zooks marched joyfully behind their King.

Chapter 12

Spring Returns

*A*s Jodi walked along the broad trail with the company of Zooks, she shared their grand feeling of "school's-out-Christmas's-here-birthday-party's-coming!" She felt freed of all cares, and her feet almost danced over the smooth trail leading through the Forest toward the west. Eric, also smiling and carefree, sang as he walked by her side. Martin was not far away . . . but Martin was not so happy: He remembered that Waymond had said the Hall of the King had been destroyed.

The long, almost straight line of Zooks passed Hopesmont by noon. Martin could see Waymond pointing upward and telling the King about the battle fought there. The King turned his gaze upon Martin and smiled. Martin blushed and bowed slightly. Jodi and Eric were too busy looking at each other to notice the King's acknowledgment of their bravery.

As the King passed through the Forest, Martin saw that changes began taking place. Trees he had not noticed before were leafing out. Buds appeared, unfurled, and spread bright green leaves into the sunlight. As the Zooks trooped by, the trees bloomed and fruit appeared—peaches, apricots, pears, and cherries. By now, Martin had seen enough strange and wonderful events occur in the Land of the King not to be overly surprised—yet wonder crept into his eyes when he noticed his favorite kind of tree sprouting fruit right beside the trail. Plums! He marvelled, walking aside to pluck some.

But he hesitated, wondering if it were forbidden to eat of the King's fruit. He glanced toward the head of the column and saw Waymond nod to him with a smile. Martin grinned and picked two of the plump, red-purple plums. He polished them on his new clothes, then began to devour the plums, wishing he could sample more of the bounty of the Forest. However, he knew that could wait.

The happy army soon rounded the western foothills of Hopesmont. They came to a series of broad, grassy hills that led downward like stairsteps toward a river valley. To the children's right they could hear the sound of the river rushing over waterfalls and splashing musically from pool to pool. At one point the trail went quite close to the river, and the Zooks looked down into green, white-frothed pools between cascades. Trout swam in the calmer water—fat rainbow trout that stared up from the clear water without fear. Martin thought: *The animals and insects already are coming back, just like the fruit and flowers.*

Indeed, it was true. Jodi and the others noticed butterflies sailing in on the south wind—iridescent ones, gold spotted ones, and long-winged blue and green ones. Birds of many sorts were not far behind, and the children also began to see squirrels, raccoons, foxes, and other smaller animals of the Forest. It was then that Jodi and Martin fully understood what Obit had done, how much he had taken from the beauty of the Land or scattered with his evil power. It was also then that they remembered Reginald. Jodi hurried to catch Waymond.

"Sir?" she began. "Back in Crossingsend, when Martin and I freed Eric, Reginald stayed behind to hold off the beasts pursuing us. I'm afraid they killed him." She hung her head sadly as Waymond looked to the King. A silent understanding seemed to pass between them before Waymond turned back to Jodi and spoke.

"When the Hall of the King is restored, we will honor Reginald—and the ferryman Wharford," the magician said.

Jodi had hoped that the King would restore Keg to life, but she saw that it would not be so. She nodded and slowed her pace until Eric was again by her side. Thinking of the brave cougar who had saved their lives, she began to cry.

Eric took her hand and pressed it gently. "Don't cry; just look at the beautiful orchids," he grinned.

"Orchids?" Jodi repeated, distracted from her unhappiness.

"Sure," Eric nodded. "And lilies and roses and tulips and . . . and I don't know them all," he laughed, pointing to the various flowers springing up along the riverbank and under the shade of the Forest.

After a moment, Jodi thoughtfully said, "You know, Eric, the Land is perfectly beautiful—like its King. Is that why the Zooks come so quickly whenever they're called?"

Eric's expression became entirely serious. "We come quickly because we love the King . . . and obey him. If he asked us to give our lives for him, we would."

Jodi nodded, greatly impressed by his bravery. Immediately, she wished that she too could have the armor, shield, and sword of the King. And, after watching the ex-Sneaks for awhile, she concluded that they shared her wish: They were looking enviously at the Zooks marching proudly up the trail, singing their song and watching their King.

The column wound its way into the narrow river valley; its sides rose high to the east and west. At the north end was a beautiful, towering waterfall where the river bounced and sprayed its way down green, flower-sprinkled cliffs. Tall trees of many kinds stood along either side of the river . . . but ahead the children saw a sight that saddened them greatly. Their singing and smiles faded.

In the middle of the valley, in a scorched meadow, was a long and wide rectangular group of enormous, charred stumps. The river flowed through the center of the rectangle, and that section of the river was fouled and stagnant with algae and trash. Around the rectangle of stumps was a large, blackened scar where flowers, grass, and trees had been blasted. The devastation obviously was the work of Reeks and Stenches, Slashes and Snitches, and their master Obit.

"All right, Zooks and apprentices!" Waymond called in a clear voice. "Roll up your sleeves and do your share of the work!"

Dividing themselves into squads, the children fanned out to all parts of the ruined area. Some waded out into the shallow pools of the river and began to fish out trash—broken bottles, old food containers, and rusting junk of all kinds that the Slashes and Stenches had left. Other squads cleaned the meadow of filth and made rakes to drag away blasted tree branches and withered weeds. Still other squads went onto the slopes of the valley to clear away the brambles set growing by the sorcerer's power from the ashes of burnings.

The Westphall children joined those attacking the brambles. Soon, Jodi and Martin's faces were streaked with sweat, and they began to tire. They came together, mopping their foreheads with the tails of their new shirts. "I wonder when we can rest and eat?" Jodi asked quietly.

"I just wish we could hurry and get this work done so the Hall of the King can be rebuilt," Martin said with a sigh. "Maybe then the King and Waymond will have the Ceremony, and we'll see if we're to get armor, shields, and real swords." He glanced enviously at nearby Zooks.

"I've been wishing the same thing," Jodi said. She bent to tug with her makeshift rake at a patch of thorny brambles that was coiled like a roll of barbed wire on the ashy ground. "I'd also like to get our shoes back," she added.

They worked in silence for a while, but soon Jodi straightened and rested again. She took a deep, relaxing breath and looked toward the tall waterfall and majestic trees at the northern end of the valley. Thoughtfully, she said, "You know, Martin, the Land is so beautiful that I wish Mom and Dad could come here and meet the King."

"That's the first time you've *ever* called Richard 'Dad,' " Martin observed, sitting down cross-legged to pull a thorn from one foot.

Jodi nodded after a moment and smiled. "I guess it is, isn't it?"

"He'd be glad," Martin commented, standing again. "Just like both of them *would* like to meet the King and see the Land—especially when we get this spot cleaned up."

"As beautiful as it is, though, and as much as I like being with the Zooks," Jodi said, leaning on her rake, "I miss being home."

"Oh, you've stayed stuck at home too much," Martin said.

"Aren't you homesick too?"

"Gosh, no!" Martin declared, then thought better of it. "Well, maybe a little. But I still want a sword and armor, and I like being with the King and having adventures with the Zooks."

"We can be with them at home, too," Jodi said, returning to work. "You know Eric, and . . ."

"Yeah," Martin grinned mischievously. "You like him, don't you?"

"Get back to work," she said abruptly, jerking at the thorn patch.

Martin snorted and went downhill to help a young Zook push a large roll of brambles to a fire that Waymond had built.

As Jodi pulled at the obstinate bramble patch, the ex-Sneak named Rachael shyly came to stand near her. "May I help you?" she asked hesitantly.

Jodi blinked and blew a sweaty strand of hair back from her eyes. "You surely may! These things just *won't* come loose!"

They introduced themselves, then set their rakes side by side. In unison the two girls tugged until the roots of the brambles popped out of the ashy soil. Smiling at their success, Rachael and Jodi sent the thorny brush rolling downhill toward the fire.

By sunset the valley was cleared of all the mess left by Obit's slaves. As daytime faded into a quiet twilight, the tired children sat down to rest. They watched the King go toward the southern end of the valley. When he had gone from sight, many of the Zooks lay back, talking quietly with one another. The darkening blue sky became streaked with rose- and orange-colored clouds. A fragrant breeze swept up the river, and night birds began weaving their tunes into the breeze. Moths fluttered from hiding places under leaves. They drifted to white, blooming moonvines that opened their long, trumpet-like flowers as the moon rose over the eastern wall of the valley. Then, the King returned.

He was not alone. With him walked a herd of tall-antlered deer. On the tips of the leaders' antlers were candles whose flames flickered in the night breeze. Behind them came other stags, and on their antlers were huge, wooden trays. As the latter deer gently lowered their heads, Zooks took down the trays and found that they were laden with all kinds of food. Then, Martin had his wish—to sample the bounty of the Land. The children comfortably feasted as they listened to the music of the river and the night birds calling.

That night, the Zooks slept on the soft meadow grass that was growing back in the burned place as the King walked upon it. It seemed the King never rested and that he walked all night among the children to give them pleasant dreams. When they awoke in the dawn's rosy-yellow glow, they felt as fresh as the flowers springing up all across the valley. And for many, their first sight upon awakening was a nearby flower, dotted with dewdrops that made tiny rainbows when touched by light from the rising sun.

As the Zooks stirred about and washed in the cool, clear water of the river, more food was brought by the herd of deer. With the deer came other animals—great shambling bears, badgers grumbling with the earliness of their awakening, tame wolves, and birds carrying strands of ivy in their beaks. With the more ordinary animals frolicked a band of what appeared to be clowns, though in fact they were coonets. Three of the coonets were more strange and comical than the rest, for they each had tennis shoes upon their hind feet. Martin gave a cry of surprise and ran to the coonet that had his shoes.

Jodi and Eric had little trouble reclaiming their

footwear, but the coonet wearing Martin's sneakers was reluctant to give up its prizes. It led Martin on a merry chase around and over the meadow before he tackled it and untied his shoes. He slipped them onto his feet and snorted at the coonet. It sort of snickered and licked his face with its extraordinarily long tongue. It then raced off to join in the game of chase the other animals were playing with the children.

"Now, my friends," the King called from higher on the slopes of the western side of the valley, "please gather along either side of the river while Waymond goes to work upon the Hall."

The animals went south as the Zooks came together. Waymond cleaned the tip of his staff and levelled it at the stump dotted meadow. Yellow lightning blazed forth and flashed here and there. From the enormous, charred stumps on each side of the river, sprouts appeared; the sprouts grew into oak, sycamore, and laurel trees, and they shot upward. In minutes, the oaks in the rectangle were thirty, then fifty, then a hundred or more feet tall. Their branches reached over the river and sprouted a multitude of leaves to form an arched roof for the Hall.

Birds planted ivy strands by the trunks of the outermost trees. Touched by the brilliant lightning from Waymond's staff, the ivy strands spiralled upward and twined across to other trees. The ivy soon formed walls of dark green leaves fluttering in the breeze. The meadow flowers within the Hall raced higher, layer upon layer. They formed colorful inner walls.

Inside the Hall—which was the size of a cathedral—aisles of short grass ran along each bank of the river and along each wall. Between the aisles, the emerald green grass—already lush and thick—grew taller to form many rows of benches. Near the front of the Hall, grassy hummocks grew long and shaped themselves into tables; the blades of grass bent flat at the tops of the tables to form a solid surface.

The river continued its musical passage down the middle of the Hall; it flowed in between twin ranks of white-barked sycamore trees that formed the northern doors. It flowed out the south end between laurel trees; those trees grew curving to form an enormous throne. The river purled directly underneath the throne. In front of the throne was a moss-covered bridge of closely spaced laurel limbs.

When the Hall had finished growing under the yellow lightning of Waymond's staff, the King descended the slope. He stopped at the huge, branch-formed doorway and turned to face the army of children that was coming along the riverbanks. Raising his hands, he said: "This Hall, for as long as it has stood, has been called the Hall of the King. Recently, however, two of us were slain while protecting the Land. Therefore, from this day on, this place of peace shall be called Reginald-Wharford Hall." The children stood silently until the King lowered his arms. Then he turned and solemnly went through the portal into the Hall. Along both sides of the river, the Zooks, ex-captives, and ex-Sneaks followed him inside.

Sunlight filtering through the leafy, green ceiling and walls made the interior light hazy and soft. The thick, oak tree trunks and branches looked like the columns and ribs of a building, though it was, of course, no ordinary structure. Here, the breeze blew freely through, and butterflies wafted in and out. Here, the sounds were not the harsh echoes of bootsteps on cold stone floors, but, rather, the purling and splashing of the gentle river. Leading the twin processions of children, the King went to the southern end of the Hall. He mounted his laurel-branch throne over the center of the river and seated himself on the boughs. He smiled pleasantly to the children on the left and right riverbanks as they settled themselves on the soft, grass benches.

When all the company was in place, the King motioned for Waymond to stand before him. When Waymond had come onto the bridge, the King and he closed their eyes. The soft, white flame that surrounded the King grew in brightness. It became so bright that the children were forced to close their eyes. Dazzling rays of purest light shone round the Hall, then seemed to sink within the King. When the children were able to look at him again, they saw that a crown of sunlight graced his golden-brown hair. The children caught their breaths in amazement, for now the King was even more radiant and regal than before. He was still the kind, loving man he had been, but now he also was a figure of awesome power and majesty.

With gentleness and restraint he began to speak. "As most of you know, we yearly conduct the Ceremony of the Upraised Swords. During that ceremony we transfer to adult service those Zooks who have reached maturity, and we install apprentices as full-fledged Zooks. This year, however, there will be a change. Magician Waymond has informed me that at least one of you has a new idea: you wish to be called Kingsmen." A murmur of children's voices expressed approval of the suggestion, so the King resumed his speech. "Therefore, Kingsmen—which includes the ladies present—form the honor guard, lift your swords high, and prepare to bid farewell to sixteen who will no longer be among us here." The King stood and called out the names of those to be honored.

There was a rustling of feet upon turf as the honor guard moved to the aisles alongside each riverbank. There was a rattling of swords against scabbards as the many shining blades were drawn and lifted high to form an archway. Sixteen shyly smiling Kingsmen one by one left their places and made their way under the upraised swords to the bridge before the throne. There, they knelt.

The King closed his eyes and held his right hand over them as they bowed their heads. "You go now," he said softly but distinctly, "into the world as adults. Although you will not again have the magicians' protection or be called here to defend the Land, remember that your armor, shields, and swords will remain with you. Remember also that it is your privilege to live in the manner you have learned as Zooks and that you will forever be . . . Kingsmen!"

The young adults before him rose and returned to their places. Jodi and Martin watched them and noted how happy they were and how confidently they carried themselves. Jodi wondered when her and Martin's turn before the King would come. Her sense of anticipation rose.

The King spread his arms toward the company and said, "Now, Kingsmen, prepare to welcome into our midst the ex-captives, who bravely withstood the sorcerer's power, and the ex-slaves of darkness who accepted our invitation."

As the restored children hurried forward to the bridge, Jodi let out her held breath and frowned slightly. In her thoughts was mild resentment that the ex-Sneaks were called before she and Martin were. But the King caught her eye with a fixating gaze. Her feeling of resentment shrivelled, and she relaxed to watch the ceremony.

"Waymond," the King called, sitting upon his throne.

The magician, polishing his staff with one hand, looked at the smiling children before him. In a clear, strong voice he declared, "For the goodness you former captives kept brightly in your hearts despite all evil, for the hope you former slaves maintained of regaining a shining name, we do here endow you with the arms and armor of the King!" He slowly swung his staff over their bowed heads; a curtain of sparkling yellow light trailed from the tip of the staff. In the wake of the light, the ex-captives and ex-Sneaks appeared in shining armor, each with a shield and a sword. Quickly, they looked at themselves and at one another; then they joyously looked at Waymond and the King. While the honor guard and audience cheered, the new Kingsmen knelt before the King. He touched each of them before they went back to their places.

The cheering stopped when the King stepped forward and again raised his hands. "Now, please prepare to welcome into our company two apprentices who have proven their worth beyond question."

As heads and eyes turned toward Jodi and Martin, they both suddenly felt unworthy. But they plainly saw the look of love and acceptance in the King's eyes. Slowly, they stood, looking at the King beyond the silver tunnel of upraised swords.

The King's strong, gentle voice carried throughout the Hall: "To be endowed with the armor of the King, to be blest with guidance to do right, let the two who have met the test come forward!" Jodi's and Martin's hearts began beating fast as Eric urged them on their way.

Looking mainly at their feet, the brother and sister began to walk along the grassy aisle of the western riverbank. As they went they heard Kingsmen murmur, "Well done!" "Good job!" "Welcome!"

Jodi thought that if only she'd *known* that the King's love and armor were to be her reward, she'd have told

Obit to jump in a lake! Martin, for his part, was simply glad to be near the King and at last to be given armor, a shield, and a sword—a real sword—of his own. He wished he had had it earlier in the adventure . . . but, he thought with a shy grin, better late than never.

When they arrived at the middle of the bridge and stood before the throne, the King motioned for them to kneel. He beckoned to Waymond, who, with some difficulty, pulled two suits of highly polished armor from his carpetbag. He laid the armor on the moss of the bridge and produced from his bag two round, sturdy shields and two very finely wrought swords, each about three feet long. He handed the light, delicately engraved armor, shields, and swords to the King.

The King nodded with satisfaction, stepped down from his throne, and proceeded to dress the children in the suits of armor. They stood with their heads bowed, embarrassed that the King himself would condescend to dress them. But, glancing at his radiant face, they saw that he actually liked serving them.

When the King had fitted the armor on them, slung their shields on their backs, and hung the swords at their sides, he gazed into their eyes. The crown of light upon his head pulsed brightly while with his look he once again filled them with love and strength. Then he turned them around to face the audience. Instantly the company of Kingsmen lifted their swords straight into the air and delivered a resounding cheer of welcome. Jodi could not keep from crying, so marvelous was it all. Martin was filled with pride, but he soon learned that the close fitting armor would not allow him to swell too big. He smiled nonetheless, feeling very grown-up.

When Jodi and Martin had gone back to sit beside Eric, the King lifted his hands over the Kingsmen one

final time. "You who are new Kingsmen, please re-
peat your oath of office after me: 'I will let the light of
my strength . . . shine for all to see . . . not in my
words . . . but in my deeds!' " When the newcomers
had finished repeating the oath, a prolonged cheer
arose from all present.

Thus, as with all adventures, this one came to a
close. A great banquet was held in the front of
Reginald-Wharford Hall during the remainder of the
day. Satisfied and strengthened, the company of
Kingsmen then began to go their separate ways. Jodi
and Martin lingered until almost all the other youthful
warriors had departed. They lingered with a growing
sadness that they would have to leave the Land and,
worse than that, that they would have to leave the
King.

He slowly descended from his green bough throne
and came toward the brother and sister, who stood
with Waymond and Eric. The King seemed to read
Jodi and Martin's thoughts as he knelt and enfolded
them in his arms. He drew them close to his warm,
soft robe and held them reassuringly within the glow
of the white flame that surrounded him.

"I don't want to leave you," Jodi whispered, wiping
her tears with trembling fingers.

"Me neither," Martin added, dabbing one fist at the
silvery drops on his cheeks. "Couldn't we just stay
and fight for you here?"

The King wiped their tears with gentle fingers and
kissed each of them. "No," he said softly but firmly.
"Although I love you dearly, there are those in your
world who love you too. You must return, else they
mourn for you."

The children silently leaned against him, feeling the
warmth and power of enduring love radiating from

196

him. Looking down at themselves, they saw that they were enveloped in his white radiance, a warm light they wished never to leave.

"But . . . ," Jodi began, looking up into his deep brown eyes.

He gently put a forefinger to her lips, then lifted her chin so her head was straight and high. Tenderly he said, "For now, your strength and knowledge are needed more in your world than here. Your call for now is there. Will you answer it for me?"

Martin sniffled, leaning closer to the King. "You mean, we should help the children who might become . . . slaves of darkness?"

The King nodded slowly. "Go now," he murmured, standing and laying a hand on each of their heads, "and keep your shields and swords ready!" He smiled to them, then turned to Waymond and Eric. "Magician Waymond and Lieutenant Ric, will you please accompany these new Kingsmen to their home?"

Both Eric and Waymond bowed slightly. "Yes, my Lord," the magician said, winking one bright brown eye at Jodi and Martin. "Gladly."

Slowly, the quartet left the Hall and made their way south down the musical river. Frequently, they turned to wave to the King, who had come into the meadow and was standing among the flowers by the silver-green river.

The journey, though long, was delightful for Jodi and Martin. Now, they felt no dread, no approaching danger, no unnerving uncertainty. Now, they felt warm and secure in their armor and in their knowledge of the King. And now the Forest was more beautiful than they had imagined it could be when they first journeyed through it. Animals and birds came to the winding, flower-bordered trail and watched the children pass. Jodi even got to see the gray eagle that she had cared for; it circled overhead for a long while, happily calling down to her.

As they walked, Eric watched Jodi, greatly pleased that she was enjoying herself and looked so pretty. Later, Eric and Waymond pointed out some of the landmarks familiar to Kingsmen from the world over, and never had Jodi seen Eric happier than when he was able to share with her what he knew of the Land.

"The river we're following," Eric explained, "is the Dain, one of five that leads to or from the Great River, which is the outer boundary of the King's Land. A northern branch of the Dain empties into the Alamantian Ocean, across which, to the north in the world of Eorthe, is the desert land of Gueroness. Remember about the Dain and Great rivers so that if—or when—the call comes again, you can make your own way into the Land."

Nightfall came as they rested atop a prairie hill overlooking the Great River. In the distance far to the south the children could see the twinkling cluster of lights that marked the location of a city.

"Is that home?" Martin asked, feeling as though he had been on a journey lasting many years.

"Yes, it is," Waymond replied, leading them down to the fording place near the junction of the Dain and Great rivers.

A kindly but silent old man with a huge round belly appeared from a bark hut near the ford. He lit a lantern, slung it at the top of a tall staff, and took each of the children in turn upon his shoulders. One by one, he carried them safely to the other side of the river. Waymond waded across behind Eric, who was carried last. Then, they watched the old man go slowly back toward his hut. Waymond waved once to the aged figure, and the lantern swung back and forth as a farewell before it was extinguished.

"Who was he?" Martin asked.

"That," the magician answered, "is old Michael, one of the ferrymen of the boundary. If—or when—you are called to return, you may meet him or others. Even though they're quiet old folk, they all truly enjoy helping children."

Jodi led the way up the riverbank, through willow thickets, and climbed a short hill. From there she began walking quickly toward the cluster of lights, eager to get home.

With a twinkle of moonlight in his eyes, Waymond asked, "What's the hurry, Miss Jodi?"

She stopped, turned, and laughed. "I can't wait to tell Mom and Dad about the King and show them my. . . ." Looking down at herself, she noticed that her suit of armor, her shield, and her polished sword had become invisible. Patting herself in several places, she looked very puzzled. "I can feel them, but . . . ."

"The King's armor, shield, and sword are still with you," Eric assured her, "and you still have their protection." He looked sadly at Waymond. "I miss mine, you know?"

Waymond nodded, then lifted his eyebrows and one finger and smiled. "That reminds me," he began, stooping to open his carpetbag and dig inside it. He pulled forth Jodi's and Martin's packs and handed them to the sister and brother. "I believe you'll need these."

"Oh, boy!" Martin exclaimed. "Now we won't get in trouble for losing our things." He squinched his mouth and looked sorrowfully up at the magician. "I'm sorry for disobeying."

The magician briefly closed his eyes and wagged one finger. "It's been taken care of. Look inside your packs, and you'll find your lights, too. Like armor, shields, and swords, the King's lights can be very useful!"

Jodi and Martin checked their lights, then slung their packs on their backs and happily walked on. Eric hurried to catch up with Jodi. Waymond and Martin smiled to each other when they saw Eric begin holding one of Jodi's hands.

The fields and pastures swelled high and fell low, and the city lights alternately dipped from view and reappeared closer and closer as the group travelled. Soon, Waymond and the hastening children were in the outskirts of the town.

Straight down the streets the children and their guide proudly walked. Shortly, they came to Eric's home. Waymond and Martin went on a bit, and Martin grinned as he glanced back to see Eric and Jodi lightly kiss good-night. With a wave to Eric, Jodi then ran to join Martin. From there the brother and sis.er raced home.

"MOM! DAD!" Jodi cried as she burst through the doorway.

"Oh, good! The kids are home!" came their mother's voice. She emerged from the kitchen and seemed greatly relieved to see that they were all right. "Where have you two been?" she asked. "I'm afraid you missed supper, but I can . . ."

"Didn't you find our note?" Martin interrupted. He unslung and dropped his pack, then ran to hug his mother with all his strength.

She laughed and kissed the top of his head. "Yes, we found your funny note. But we thought you were just joking—especially about the magician. You were . . . weren't you?"

Before the children could think how to answer her, their stepfather came from the rear of the house. Jodi set her pack on the floor and ran into his arms—much to his surprise. He warmly hugged her in return. Next, he went to shake Martin's hand in a grown-up way that seemed to fit Martin's new manner, then hugged him too. "Have a good adventure?" he asked.

"Yes, sir!" Martin declared. "We had a *fine* adventure!"

"Well?" their mother asked, her eyebrows lifted. "Where's this magician? I'd like to meet him."

"Waymond!" Jodi called, running to the still-open front door. "Waymond?" She looked into the dark night outside . . . but found that he had gone. As she slowly returned to her family, tears came into her eyes.

"Don't worry," Martin whispered to her. "I'm sure the Kingsmen will be called again. Then we'll see him."

Jodi wiped her tears, smiling at her parents. She burst out, "Oh, Mom, Dad, we met the most wonderful person—the King! I wish you could meet him and see where he lives!"

"A king?" her mother asked doubtfully. She went to sit down.

The children sat facing their parents. They took turns telling all that had happened, ignoring their parents' half-skeptical, half-believing looks. Jodi and Martin ended by showing them their lights and by telling about the armor, shields, and swords.

After a moment of silence, their perplexed mother said, "Oh, my . . . well, I do like your candlestick and flashlight and your new green clothes . . . and the fact that I've never seen you happier."

Jodi and Martin smiled hugely at each other.

Their stepfather came and kissed each of them.

"With or without new clothes and lights, I can tell that something wonderful has happened to you. I'm glad—and thankful. And I'd love to meet your king!"

"Me too," their mother agreed, wiping her eyes as she smiled at her children.

Jodi burst into tears of joy and ran with Martin to hug them both.

Late that night, while her parents slept contentedly, Jodi lay awake in her bedroom. "Martin?" she whispered loudly.

In his room across the hall, Martin, too, was still awake, thinking about all that had happened. "Yes?" he whispered back.

"Are you listening for the call?" Jodi whispered.

"You bet I am," came the reply.

"Will you wake me if you hear it and I've gone to sleep?" Jodi asked.

Martin laughed. "Sure, if you'll do the same for me."

"Okay," she whispered, closing her eyes. "Just listen for the call!"

The End

In *Lightning in the Bottle*, the second book of *The Legends of Eorthe*, Eric, Jodi, Martin, skeptical cousin Richard, the Waif, and Rachael answer the call of the Horn of Meet to find the Land of the King in winter and their purpose far beyond. They must cross the Alamantian Ocean and the desert continent of Gueroness to help Morgan Evnstar, son of King Mervintide, save his ocean-island kingdom of Alamantia. The threat comes from the dark forces of Jabez and Sarx, sorcerer sons of Ingloamin, Lord of Darkness, for whom Obit is merely a servant. Another of the King's magicians, Acuerias, leads the Kingsmen to rescue the power of peace—the LIGHTNING IN THE BOTTLE.